Izzie and

CW00973039

After her fur-raisi

highly trained, sassy, specialist space dog, is working on a spaceship that transports rare, precious metals from asteroid mines. Her Top Dog is Dixie, the ship's scientific and security officer. Disturbing events start after they leave the Moon. First, there's the explosion of the ship which her twin, Dan, works on. Then their own ship is sabotaged. When they arrive at the asteroid to pick up their cargo, they find someone has been stealing secrets. Dixie and Izzie investigate. But who is behind these criminal events? What is their motive? Can Izzie help solve the puzzle before it is too late? Just who can she trust? And what, exactly, has happened to Dan?

Royalties are donated to Hearing Dogs for Deaf People.

To Rafty

Enjoy!

Mike Mon

Izzie and the Space Pirates

Dedicated to my Pack and all Hearing Dogs
and those who love them. Woof!

Me, in my spacesuit.

By the same author (available from Amazon Books)

A Small Dog Story

Izzie and the Martian Adventure

Published by Mike Moss 2020

THIS ADVENTURE

Chapter 1 – Lunar Orbiter Alpha

A dog? In space, you ask? And why not? Dogs went into space before people. The Russian cosmodogs Laika, once a stray like me[1], and Belka and Strelka took trips into space before the first cosmonaut, Yuri Gagarin. So it's no coincidence that, one hundred years later, the brand new, shiny spaceship I am on is called Space Barge Yuri Gagarin. Our ship belongs to Astromin, the galactic mining company, and will carry rare and precious 'technology' metals from the asteroid mines back to Earth. Supplies on Earth are running short, due to decades of poor recycling, so these metals are desperately needed for smart phones, tablets, computers and the internet of things.

You find us preparing our ship for its maiden voyage whilst docked at Lunar Orbiter Alpha, the largest space station orbiting the Moon.

I should point out that I'm not just any dog. I'm a really useful, highly trained, specialist space dog with a super-charged sniff (and I have, with all modesty, a medal to prove it). I was second in my year at the Space

[1] See 'A Small Dog Story' for Izzie's puppy adventures.

Dog Academy, Alfie the Alsatian beat me by a whisker. I'm trained to use my intelligence in difficult situations, find smugglers and, as we live in dangerous times, search for explosives, bombs and stolen metals (I'm also very good at finding food). There are plenty of global companies, foreign powers and criminals who would like to disrupt the asteroid mining programme. As I'm a terrier I can also catch rats and chase small, furry animals, though there aren't many of these in space. Because I'm grey and quite shaggy, some people think I'm an Ewok from Star Wars, which is a bit daft as they are from a galaxy far, far away.

You find me on duty with Ruff, my robotic pet squirrel, sitting patiently behind me. I'm helping my owner and friend Dixie. Dixie oversees security and safety on our ship. She also manages our science experiments and is our medic (and occasionally vet). She is personable, professional and always neat and tidy. Take it from me, I think you would like her if you met her. I adore her. She is my top dog.

We had been loading our final stores, food, equipment and passengers, before heading off to the asteroid Thisbe to pick up our cargo of metals. Now, standing by the door at the top of the space station boarding ramp, I could hear our last passenger arriving before he turned the corner. Dixie rubbed a crease from her neatly fitting grey overalls and checked her gravity boots were still shiny. Our passenger walked, or rather limped, up the ramp. Dixie studied her list. I looked up and took in his features. Shorter than Dixie, stout, his bald head offset by the shaggiest black eyebrows I had ever seen. I wondered if there were any unknown lifeforms living in them.

'Doctor Zolotov, I presume?' asked Dixie. The man frowned.

'Correct, and you are, ah, the security officer,' he replied in a thick Russian accent, taking in Dixie's name badge, then looking her straight in the eyes with a stare that cooled the corridor. He smiled, then looked down at me, 'And you have a dog, how unusual.'

'I'm a highly trained, specialist space dog,' I woofed. I don't think he noticed the 'Above and Beyond' medal hanging from my collar. I was proud to be the first dog ever to be earn this medal, awarded for helping save the Galileo Base on Mars from Sun Tzu and his ghastly galactic gang.[2]

---

[2] See 'Izzie and the Martian Adventure' for Izzie's fur-raising adventure on Mars.

'Yes, Doctor, that's Izzie. Please scan your thumb print here to verify identification.'

Zolotov, looking a little tense, placed his thumb on the reader, which turned green and beeped.

'Thank you, now place your bag in the scanner, please.'

I sensed Zolotov relax. He removed his rucksack and put it on the scanner table. The circular scanner twirled around the bag, stopped and glowed green. Dixie lifted the rucksack, opened it and held it low for me to sniff. I could smell traces of laundry powder (well-known brand), aftershave, metals consistent with a tablet device, a few other normal smells, Chinese food (king prawns in chilli oyster sauce) but nothing to report to Dixie. I sat down and wagged my tail, the 'all clear' sign.

'Thank you, Doctor. You're the last passenger. Here is your cabin key, number six. It's just down the passenger corridor on the left. We'll be leaving in an hour or so,' explained Dixie. 'We have a few last-minute supplies to load then we're off to Thisbe via Mars. I understand you will be leaving us at the Mars Orbiter space station before continuing to Titan.' Zolotov nodded. Dixie continued, 'When you have checked into your room please go straight to the passenger lounge and start the safety and orientation briefing. There are five other passengers on board.'

Zolotov nodded and picked up his rucksack. 'Number six, on the left you say, thank you.'

I watched Doctor Zolotov limp away. The hairs on the back of my neck tingled a warning. Something was odd. Maybe it was his false smile. Maybe it was a Russian who liked Chinese food. My thoughts were interrupted as Dixie turned to close the door. It slid closed and clicked shut.

'Right, Izzie,' my ears pricked up, 'All six passengers on board. I'll call Jules or Smithy to check we've loaded that last-minute equipment for Thisbe.'

Jules and Smithy were the crew technicians who looked after loading, cargo, general maintenance and all the odd jobs that needed doing. They would be below on the cargo deck, dealing with the final items. Dixie pressed the radio button on her belt.

'Dixie to Jules or Smithy, come in.' A pause, a bit of crackle caused by solar wind radiation.

'Hi, Dixie, how's it going? All passengers aboard?'

'Hi, Jules, yup, all aboard. How's that gear for the Thisbe mine coming on?'

A woman's voice chipped in, Smithy. 'Just finished locking it down, so the front cargo deck is all secure,' she chimed in her sing song voice.

'Rear deck is secure,' added Jules.

'Well done, team. I'll tell the Captain.' Dixie checked the boarding door was secure and turned to me. 'Come on, Izzie, off to the flight deck.'

I picked up Ruff. As usual, he whirred and wriggled then squeaked in alarm. This was exciting, my second space voyage was about to start! Hopefully no-one would try to blow us up this time!

Chapter 2 – Into Outer Space

Dixie strode purposefully down the crew corridor towards the flight deck. I caught up and took the lead. The walls were decorated with large pictures of famous space events. First was a smiling Yuri Gagarin about to board his rocket. Next was John Glenn, the first American to orbit Earth, talking to Katherine Johnson, who hand checked the calculations for his return. Then it was Neil Armstrong, taking his first step on the moon, saying 'That's one small step for man, one giant leap for mankind', closely followed by his companion Buzz Aldrin. A few more and we reached a mural depicting the first colony on Mars, Galileo Base, set up by a team led by Dixie's parents. I knew Dixie felt a surge of pride whenever she saw the picture of her parents standing outside the base, their faces partially obscured by their helmet visors. They had always taught us to be the best we can be and to seize life's opportunities. Like their parents, Dixie and Dan were naturally gifted, and now they were on fast track careers with Astromin. She stopped to blow them a kiss, her way of dealing with her loss, anger and frustration. They had died on Mars when their ship crashed on take-off, sabotaged by Sun Tzu and his gang. To our frustration, Sun had escaped in a shuttle at the last minute and was now a hunted criminal. Dixie and her twin Dan had vowed to bring him to justice and make him pay for his crimes. I don't think she would ever forgive him. Her parents had been space heroes, so much so that the next space barge to be built was to be named after them.

The pictures were interspersed by silver doors leading to the crew cabins, the engineering control room, the kitchen, and the canteen shared with the passengers. I paused to sniff the air. T'unc, our chef, was cooking a chicken tikka, Smithy's favourite. Maybe, I thought, that's why Smithy had married him a few months ago on this very space station. Opposite the canteen was the crew gym, essential to help maintain fitness in space and reduce muscle wastage in our low gravity environment. Alongside the gym was the crew lounge with its digital library of games, books, films and shows, and its comfy chairs. I knew they were comfy; I had tried them all when no-one was looking.

We approached the flight deck. On the right was the door to Dixie's cubicle, her 'office' which she shared with the Captain. Straight ahead, the main door to the flight deck quietly swooshed open as I approached. My collar tag opens all the main doors[3]. Dixie swept along behind me. We entered an ultra-modern star barge flight deck. The front and side walls were one huge screen, built using nanotechnology. Currently split up into sections, it showed three dimensional images of the engines, green and amber lights, layouts of the ship and live camera shots of the cargo deck and the space dock. The screen was so large that when Eva, our pilot, was alone on the flight deck, she would switch the display to tranquil, life size wraparound scenes. Her favourite was a lake surrounded by forested mountains, the waters lapping lazily against a sandy beach. It reminded her of her favourite place on Earth. It was so real I nearly walked into it the first time I saw it. Smithy made us all laugh when she programmed the file to make a huge dinosaur amble out of the wood, take a drink, turn around and run at Eva. She jumped a foot into the air.

---

[3] Once, when I was little, Dixie took me to a pet museum and showed me a similar, antique collar from the year 2005 that allowed cats into their house through a little door. The little door would only open if the right cat, wearing the right collar, tried to jump through.

In the centre of the flight deck was a console with six smaller, TV sized touchscreens, all showing data in various colours. Three high backed chairs stood in front, empty.

The Captain was talking urgently to Eva. His shiny bald head reflected the ceiling lights. He was stroking his grey beard, a habit of his, whilst pointing to a flashing red light on the wall screen. Eva was puzzling over something on her tablet.

'OK, Captain, I don't think it was caused by the algorithm upgrade. I'll go check it out,' concluded Eva, turning to leave. 'Hi, Dixie,' she added as she walked past. She patted me. I wagged my tail.

'Hi, Eva.' Dixie turned to report. 'All passengers aboard, all cargo loaded and secure, Captain.'

The Captain nodded. 'Thanks, Dixie. We have a problem with the rear airlock switch, it's showing up as open. Eva's gone to find Mo or Smithy to fix it.'

Mo was the ship's chief engineer, responsible for all the equipment and maintenance. We had worked with her when we saved the Mars Galileo Base from the evil criminal, Sun Tzu. She was a no-nonsense person who could fix things in no time with the help of her team, Jules and Smithy.

I settled down in my basket next to Dixie's desk to watch as the Captain and Dixie continued to carefully scan the wall screens to confirm everything was ready to go. After all, this was our first deep space flight.

A short while later, the intercom crackled into life. 'Captain, Eva here. The door switch is fixed, should be showing green.'

'Thanks, Eva,' replied the Captain as Dixie checked the wall screen.

'That's confirmed,' added Dixie, 'It's green now.'

'Back to the flight deck then please Eva,' ordered the Captain.

Eva soon reappeared and took the right hand of the three chairs. The Captain took the middle chair whilst Dixie sat in the empty chair. She smoothed her short blond hair. It used to be shoulder length but, after her parents were murdered, she had cut it short, almost elfin like. She never explained why.

Eva switched to the ladar screen. Ladar is an acronym for LAser Detection And Rangefinding. It beams variable frequency laser light all around the ship in regular, split second pulses, then maps their reflection. It allowed objects as small as an acorn to be seen, essential for a ship travelling at 600,000 kilometres per hour (which is very, very fast[4]). Not that you would find many acorns in space but, at that speed, an asteroid the size of an acorn could do serious damage.

'All clear, Captain,' confirmed Eva.

'OK, everyone, buckle up!' commanded the Captain.

Dixie turned to check on me, but I knew the drill. I didn't have a belt, so I had to lie back in my special padded basket, moulded to my shape, which itself was secure against the partition between the flight deck and Dixie's desk. I took a last lick of water from my yellow bowl, labelled K9 H2O, then wriggled backwards into my basket.

'Here we go, then,' the Captain announced. 'Lunar Orbiter Alpha control, this is Space Barge Yuri Gagarin, we are ready to launch.'

'Roger that, Yuri Gagarin, you have clearance to leave. Safe journey,' came the reply.

The Captain typed in the launch code. A quiet hum filled the air as the engine started. There was a slight

---

[4] Izzie is quite right. At that speed you could fly from the Earth to the Moon <u>and back</u> in the same time it takes an average Londoner to commute to work each day!

jolt as the docking cradle disengaged and the launch engine pushed us gently away from the dock.

Eriko, the space station commander, sitting in her control tower, would have had a clear view of our ship. She would have admired the sleek outline, its rounded nose sloping back to a flattened cylinder, picked out by a double row of lighted windows. At the back of the ship, the ion drive's exhaust gas glowed, leaving a faint emerald green trail. Two huge cargo containers were slung underneath, supplies for Mars and Thisbe. Slowly the ship eased away from the space station, slipping sideways across the sea of stars. Five minutes later we were well clear of the dock and the Captain reached for the intercom.

'We are about to switch to the main ion drive. Please remain in your seats until I get back to you, in about an hour. We will be accelerating quickly so you will feel some G force, but no worse than a roller coaster ride.'

He tapped another code into the screen. A faint, lower frequency hum started, and I was thrust back into my basket by the acceleration. This part of space flight always made me feel queasy, especially if I shut my eyes. In an hour, the Captain would reduce acceleration, but it would still take a day to reach our cruising speed of 600,000 kilometres per hour. Even at that speed it would take a week to reach our first destination, Mars Orbiter, the space station orbiting the fourth planet from the Sun.

Dixie saw me tensing. 'Relax, Izzie, try practising those mindfulness techniques we learnt.'

So I 1thought about treats and chasing squirrels. I like to chase them when Dixie takes me to the park on Earth. Of course, there aren't any squirrels on a spaceship, except Ruff. I know this because Dixie told me. Even so, I searched the whole ship, just in case she was wrong. She wasn't.

Once we were allowed out of our seats, I decided to take a tour of the ship, even though I was a little unsteady on my feet. It wasn't long before my tummy told me it was lunchtime, so I went to visit T'unc in the kitchen. Smithy was there. She would often help him out in the kitchen. I found them scrubbing the stainless steel surfaces and polishing the pristine pots and pans. You could feel T'unc's passion in the way he ran his kitchen and served up his dishes. Long gone were the days astronauts ate food out of tubes. T'unc was equally passionate and proud about his twin nephew and niece. He was always singing their praises. That's how he earned his nickname, T'unc, short for The Uncle. The twins had signed up as apprentice technicians with Astromin and had recently started working on Lunar Orbiter Alpha.

I entered the kitchen and sat next to the door, in my usual corner, slowly wagging my tail. It wasn't a large kitchen, big enough to cook for about fifteen people, lots of cupboards, ovens, hobs and a huge superfast dishwasher. A big door opened into a walk-in refrigerator and another into a freezer room. A large hatch opened onto the canteen area, where crew and passengers ate together.

You wouldn't find a better, kinder cook than T'unc on any of the star ships serving the mines, but I knew better than to distract him when he was immersed in his art of cooking. It wasn't long before T'unc looked up from his chopping board.

'Smithy, have you fed Izzie?' he called, pushing a strand of his newly dyed ginger hair under his cook's cap. He had dyed it to match Smithy's natural colour, just after they were married. Smithy poked her head out from behind the hob.

'Hi, Izzie, be with you in a minute,' she smiled. I wagged my tail a little faster.

Chapter 3 – A Mysterious Leg

Life soon assumed the routine of space flight. Most things look after themselves on a super-sophisticated ship like ours. Artificial intelligence, running on the ship's supercomputer, made this possible. The crew were a good team, having worked on preparing the ship for three months. The passengers were mixing well. At least, most of them. Dr Zolotov seemed to keep himself to himself. Apart from Dr Zolotov there were three other men, replacement crew for the Galileo Base on Mars. They were all in their twenties; Joe, a gregarious geologist, Baz, a super brainy, serious looking doctor from Nigeria, glasses perched precariously on his nose, and Jamie who, it turned out, was a talented chef and loved to swap recipes with T'unc. He even helped in the kitchen, which went down well with Smithy. The other two passengers were women, both on their way to the mine on Thisbe, the asteroid where we would collect our cargo of precious metals twelve days after leaving Mars. Jas was a mining engineer and astrobiologist who spent most of the time smiling and laughing. She told us that Astromin were trialling new bacteria to help digest the metal ore on Thisbe. This would produce purer metal at the mine. Françoise was from Quebec, where she qualified as an IT and communication engineer. She was quiet and often had her headphones jammed on her head, listening to Quebecois folk songs. Jas found her a bit stand-offish but hoped to get to know her on the way to Thisbe.

First thing every morning Dixie and I went to the gym. I trotted and ran four miles on the treadmill, chasing squirrels and other furry animals that darted in and out of the screen in front of me. Dixie burned calories on the cross trainer and bike and used the weights and punchball. Her tall (I should point out that most humans look tall to a terrier), toned body gave the impression that it might be a mistake to challenge her to a fight which, incidentally, it would have been. Eriko, the station commander on Lunar Orbiter Alpha, had been running a judo class over the last three months, and Dixie had been a star pupil. After our gym session, we would have our breakfast then conduct a tour of the ship. Dixie liked to ensure everything was in order.

'Captain, would you like me to tidy your files?' she asked kindly one morning, 'Only I noticed you spent a while looking for that cargo list yesterday.'

'It's not that bad, Dixie,' replied the Captain, 'Though I suppose my filing is a bit messy.' He looked down at the nano-screen that made up his desktop, covered in digital papers, yellow digital post-its and digital folders. 'On the other hand……….,' he looked hopefully at Dixie.

'Consider it done, Captain!'

Part of my job was to keep an eye on the passengers, so I would often go into their accommodation. Usually I would find them watching a film or playing a game in the lounge, having fitness competitions in the gym or eating together in the canteen. Françoise would join in if encouraged. Zolotov was something else. He didn't mix and was a bit of an outsider. He preferred to spend most of his time in his cabin. He told Dixie he was busy doing research. Dixie looked him up on the internet and found several scientific papers he had written about extracting and refining methane gas on moons.

'It turns out our Dr Zolotov is quite an expert and world famous, Izzie,' reported Dixie one quiet afternoon, looking at her screen whilst finishing her fourth custard cream of the day. I knew it was her fourth, I can't help counting as I watch her eat. She threw a piece my way. I caught it in mid-air and ate it guiltily. I know I shouldn't eat human biscuits, they could give me toothache if I'm not careful. I don't know why Dixie never suffered from it.

'Come on,' she said, standing up, 'Time for our afternoon tour.'

We left the flight deck, first stop the kitchen. T'unc was hard at work watching Jamie chop vegetables. Dixie sniffed appreciatively.

'Hmm, smells good, what is it?'

'Beef stew', I woofed.

'Boeuf Bourguignon,' replied T'unc. Exactly what I said.

'And you have a new helper,' Dixie noted. Jamie looked up as he carried on chopping.

'I love cooking. Learnt to do it in the children's home.'

'Cool,' replied Dixie as she looked quizzically at T'unc. Orphan, he mouthed silently.

'Yup,' Jamie continued, 'I was kicked out when I reached eighteen, too old to stay. Never was very good at studying books and doing exams. Maths was a mystery, but I liked chemistry. So, I thought, what can I do? Then it hit me like a frozen snowball from space.

Cook! Cooking is like chemistry, right?' he looked up and grinned. 'I love the different tastes and smells and I enjoy working out new recipes, measuring out the ingredients, writing it all down and sharing them on the web.'

'He's good, too,' chipped in T'unc, 'A pleasure to have him in my kitchen. He'll be running a Michelin starred restaurant one day, I bet!'

Dixie smiled and turned to leave but not before Jamie threw me a piece of cheese. By now I knew the round by heart. Next stop, Mo in the engineering room. Mo spent a lot of the time on the flight deck but, at this time of day, she would be in engineering running her daily diagnostic checks. Sure enough, she was there when we entered, sitting at her console in the middle of the room, viewing data on the three screens in front of her. Her fuzz of dark hair was just visible above the back of the chair. Dixie looked over Mo's shoulder.

'All good?' she asked.

'Running like a dream,' replied Mo. 'The tune up we did in the space dock was spot on. Just a couple of tweaks needed to optimise the ion drive, that's all.'

I sniffed around. Behind the console, the wall screens displayed a diagram of the ion drive, the electrical and ventilation systems and the life support status, all good. I trotted over to the corner and looked down the spiral staircase into the engineering workshop. I could hear Jules and Smithy chatting whilst they worked on repairing a broken component. I went down a few steps. I could see the door leading to the cargo deck and the escape shuttles and, along the other wall, Jules and Smithy were standing at a workbench.

'Hi,' I woofed. They turned and smiled. Smithy came over and patted my head.

'Hi, Dixie,' she called up the staircase.

'Hi, Smithy, don't let Izzie bother you if you're busy.'

As if I would. Bother anyone I mean. I licked Smithy's nose. Dixie stayed to have a coffee with Mo and learn a little more about the ion drive. The technology was quite new, at least our version was. It had been developed by Professor Henriatti at the Astromin Space Academy (when Dixie and I were studying there, we solved the theft of his software). Our ion drive worked by turning a secret gas into electrically charged molecules, called ions. These ions are accelerated using huge magnets and sent flying backwards at ultra-high speeds, making the ship move forward. I didn't follow all of it but it's obviously very clever. I think Mo was pleased to have someone to talk to. She started asking Dixie what she missed most about being away from Earth.

'Fresh air, I think,' she replied. 'Walking Izzie on the beach, a sea breeze on my face. And a hike in the mountains, with trees and bird song, and lakes and views. And the change of seasons.'

'Chasing squirrels,' I woofed, 'That's what I miss, and running in the park.'

After a while Dixie stood up and announced it was time to continue our tour.

As we returned to the crew corridor, something caught my eye; a leg disappearing around the corner, towards the canteen. Whoever it was, they weren't wearing a grey overall, so it can't have been a crew member. As passengers weren't allowed in this corridor, I barked to alert Dixie.

'What is it, Izzie?'

I ran down the corridor. The canteen door opened but no-one was there. I sniffed the ground but there were lots of scents mixed up, many recent, one of.......

Chinese food? Well, it was a canteen, after all. Dixie caught up.

'What is it, Izzie?' she asked again. Now we specialist space dogs are trained to do many clever things, like putting paws on suspicious packages, signing if it's explosive or toxic, or telling humans we're hungry. However, we don't have any bark or sign language to say, 'I saw a suspicious person darting around the corner, but I didn't see who it was so I just woofed my alert woof'.

Dixie followed me into the canteen. It was quite small, a few tables, one secure door into the crew corridor and one door leading to the passenger corridor. Dixie crossed to the serving hatch. Leaning over, she saw T'unc and asked if he had seen anything. Too busy stirring was his reply.

Dixie frowned. We walked back into the crew corridor and entered the crew lounge. Eva was there, watching a film, relaxing on a cream coloured, comfy chair. In the corner was a drinks and snacks machine, which even included doggy treats. On the back wall were cupboards containing old games and jigsaws (one of T'unc's hobbies). Next stop was the clinic, Dixie's other office, adjacent to her cubicle. It was organised and tidy, as you would expect from Dixie, and contained floor to ceiling cupboards of medical supplies. At the far end, behind a glass wall, were two beds. Above each bed was a shelf of medical equipment and monitors. With the help of robotic equipment, using artificial intelligence, this area could be made into a quarantine room, an intensive care unit or a sterile operating theatre.

Dixie confirmed everything was in order. We went across to the passenger lounge. Françoise was there on her own, but she was totally engrossed in her headphones and paid us no notice. Next stop was the cargo deck. Much of the space was taken up with boxes, last minute items that didn't go in a container. In one corner stood the deck air lock, the main access to and from the ship once in space. On one wall were the lockers for equipment, space suits, tools and the like. Along the other side were storerooms for food and freezers. Towards the back were the batteries that stored energy from the solar cells and the equipment that sweetened the air and recycled the wastewater and other waste. At the very back was the refrigeration equipment that cooled freezers, fridges and air conditioning. Its pipes were covered in ice, like a heavy frost back on Earth, and above them, picked out by the ceiling lights, hung a small, shimmering rainbow.

Rainbows fascinated me. I remembered the story Dixie had told me about rainbows being a promise. A promise that there would be no more floods, which I thought ironic. The humans had made a dog's dinner of climate change, doing too little, too late. Now the melting ice caps meant land was being reclaimed by the sea. Dozens of cities were flooded, New York, Tokyo, Venice, Miami, Hong Kong, the list went on. Islands and homes had disappeared. Maybe it was better to be in space, I mused. At least our feet wouldn't get wet.

Once Dixie had checked the escape shuttles, our tour was finished. Back on the flight deck, I sat in my basket as Dixie conscientiously completed her report. I was still trying to work out who I might have seen in the corridor as I dozed off. Had I realised what was going to happen next, I wouldn't have slept so easily.

Chasing Squirrels in the park on Earth

Chapter 4 – The Missing Spaceship

It was on the third evening, halfway to Mars, when it happened. Dixie and I were in our cabin watching Orbit News Live on the TV. Dixie had been learning a new tune on her guitar. Now she had her feet up on her bunk and was eating a couple of custard creams and drinking her cocoa. I was sitting in my basket chewing my dentastick, the doggy equivalent of cleaning my teeth. There was a news report about a new mine opening on an asteroid called Vela, followed by an item about an invention that would help protect space travellers, and space dogs no doubt, from space radiation. The report was interrupted by breaking news about debris picked up by the Hawking space telescope. The newsreader continued…

'The incident happened near the edge of the asteroid belt that lies between Mars and Jupiter. The debris is believed to be from the Space Barge Buzz Aldrin, bound from Titan to Earth. It was carrying a full cargo of methane gas which is extracted from the largest moon…..'

Dixie sat bolt upright, spilling her drink over her slippers.

'…. of Saturn. It is believed there may be no survivors. In fact………'

'TV, stop, rewind,' commanded Dixie.

The news snippet started again. It explained that the huge cloud of debris and methane gas, believed to be from an exploding cargo barge, was expanding across the emptiness of space. The only known ship in the area had been the Space Barge Buzz Aldrin, carrying gas from Titan to Earth. Attempts had been made to contact the ship but without success. Any ships in the area were being asked to look out for escape shuttles. A ship was being sent from the nearest asteroid mine, Vela, to investigate, look for survivors and search for the ship's flight recorder.

Dixie sat stock still. I looked at her, then back to the TV and back to her, puzzled. A tear started in her eye then trickled down her cheek. Her shoulders slumped.

'Oh, Izzie, that was Dan's ship!'

Now I was shocked. Now I understood. Dan was Dixie's twin. The three of us had graduated at the

Astromin Space Academy a few months ago, the day their parents were killed on Mars.

'Izzie, that was Dan's ship! He was all I had left, my best friend,' she sobbed, sitting down next to me and putting her arm around me, 'Apart from you of course, but you're a dog.'

I understood. I nuzzled up close to her and licked a salty tear from her cheek. It was all I could do. Suddenly she sat up straight.

'Maybe he wasn't on the ship, maybe he missed it or maybe he's been rescued. We need to go and see the Captain and send a message to Astromin HQ.'

She ran out of the door, still in her pyjamas, towards the flight deck. I followed. Just as we passed the kitchen, T'unc stepped out with a tray of food. Dixie side stepped smartly and continued.

'Whoa, Dixie, what's the hurry?' called T'unc.

'Bad news,' I woofed but T'unc just shook his head and followed us to the flight deck. By the time he arrived, the Captain and Eva were watching the newscast with Dixie. Eva had her arm around Dixie's shoulder. The Captain looked grim.

'Let's be optimistic, Dixie,' he said kindly, 'There's every reason to hope that Dan managed to reach an escape shuttle in time, and people can survive in these shuttles for weeks. I'll call Astromin HQ to check the crew list and see if Dan was on board, and I'll call Titan, Mars and the mines to alert them, see what they can do to help. It sounds like the search and rescue mission has already started.'

He looked Dixie in the eye. 'Obviously we're too far away to help. We must be twelve days journey from where it happened, but we'll do all we can.'

Dixie nodded, sniffed and wiped her nose on her sleeve. That's not like her, I thought.

T'unc set down the tray. He had heard everything. He knew Dan. T'unc had been chef at the Space Academy when we were there.

'Come on, Dixie, let's go to the kitchen and have a nice cup of something. Not much we can do here.'

Dixie nodded and T'unc took her by the arm and led the way. I looked at the Captain.

'Don't you worry, Izzie. You go with Dixie.'

So I did. I followed them to the kitchen and found Dixie, sitting slumped at T'unc's little corner desk. T'unc was making a fresh pot of coffee.

'Decaf,' he said, putting down a steaming cup in front of Dixie, who cradled it in her hands. The door opened and Mo walked in. She went straight up to Dixie and put her hand on Dixie's wrist.

'The Captain just told me. I'm so sorry, but there's every chance he escaped in time.'

Dixie nodded, still too upset to say anything, and patted Mo's hand. Mo looked up at T'unc, who shrugged. I stood up and put my paws and chin on Dixie's knee to show that I cared too. She stroked my head. Mo broke the silence.

'The Captain will let us know as soon as there is any news. He's trying all channels to find out more information.'

Dixie nodded and sipped her coffee.

Again it was Mo who broke the silence. 'There's nothing you can do right now, Dixie. Why not go to bed?'

'No,' replied Dixie standing up, 'I think I'll watch the news in the lounge, just in case. Can you tell the Captain, please?'

Mo nodded. 'Sure, and I'll come and keep you company.'

Dixie reached the door and turned.

'Thanks, you two. I'm Dan's twin, I would have felt something, wouldn't I? I mean if he was…. you know…if he is…...'

Mo nodded. Dixie turned and left.

'I'll keep an eye on her, T'unc. You get to bed.'

T'unc nodded, picked up Dixie's mug, then poured another and handed it to Mo.

'Thanks, Mo, I'm not good at this sort of thing.'

Mo looked at me and nodded towards the door. 'Izzie, keep Dixie company. I'll be along in a few minutes.'

Much later, in the early hours of the morning, Mo and Dixie had finally dozed off. I lay there, watching the continuous bulletins on the Orbit News Live channel. By the time the cock would have crowed on Earth, all three of us were in a restless sleep. The TV, sensing no motion, switched itself off.

'Good morning all!' It was T'unc with coffee and bacon and sausage sandwiches. Dixie woke with a start.

'He's alive!' she exclaimed, 'I dreamt it! We're twins. We have a bond. He's alive, I'm certain.'

T'unc looked at Mo, who was still wiping the sleep out of her eyes.

'News on!' commanded Dixie to the TV.

We watched for a while, eating our breakfast (yes, OK, I had a special dog sized sausage sandwich too, what's wrong with that?). There was nothing new in the bulletins. A short while later the Captain came in, looking weary.

'No real news yet, Dixie, though Astromin have confirmed Dan was on board.' The Captain paused, 'The ship from Vela is close to the area of, er, the debris field and is scanning the region. It's too early to say if any escape shuttles were launched. Everyone is doing what they can, I promise.'

Dixie nodded, 'Thanks, Captain, I know.' She stood up. 'I'll get dressed and head to the gym. Come on, Izzie.'

With that she patted the Captain on the shoulder and we left, leaving the Captain looking forlornly at the floor.

Chapter 5 – The Comet

The rest of the morning was routine. Gym then some work. Dixie flicked through the news channels every 30 minutes, even though she had set up an automatic alert for any item about the Buzz Aldrin. We completed our usual tour of the ship. Word had spread and Dixie received some kind words from Jules, a hug from Smithy and a longer than usual coffee with Mo.

Part of Dixie's role was to conduct scientific experiments and that afternoon we had a special scientific mission to occupy us. We had been asked by a famous English university to intercept a new comet that had recently appeared in the inner Solar System. With Astromin's approval, we had slowed down and changed course slightly to fly past it. Our task was to launch two of our robotic exploration probes. The first would land on the comet and take samples of its surface. The second would follow the comet to measure the composition of its tail. A comet's tail is formed by gas and dust flying off its surface as it warms, melts and fizzes in the weak sunlight.

'Come on, Izzie,' Dixie called, 'We're slowing down. We need to prepare to launch our probes.'

I followed Dixie down to the cargo deck. Smithy had an image of the comet on the screen. All we could see was a hazy view of its tail, streaking away to the left as it was battered and pushed by the solar wind. Smithy had already unpacked the probes and they were sitting on the floor, each about the size of a shoe box.

'I've run the diagnostic checks, Dixie. No problems.'

'Thanks, Smithy. We're only going to have one shot at this, so let's run through what we have to do.'

They discussed the ship's approach and the order the probes would be released. We would steer them for a few minutes only, so the launch had to be just right. Flying through a comet's tail could be dangerous for a spaceship travelling at our speed, so the radiation shields had to be at maximum power. This would deflect the electrical particles from the comet's tail and protect us. With only 20 minutes to go, the probes were put in the airlock. Dixie monitored the approach speed and angle every minute on the computer.

'OK, open the outer airlock doors, Smithy. Ready……….' Dixie pressed the command for the first probe to shoot off into the comet's tail.

'Stabilising now,' announced Smithy, watching her computer screen. 'Looking good. Data connected, streaming now.'

A computer screen lit up with data. Dixie leant over and watched it for a minute. 'Great, that looks good. Now, second probe, ready…..'

The comet was looming large in the screen and in the portholes, completely blotting out any view of the stars. It looked like a huge, dirty snowball with hills and valleys, pitted here and there with ancient craters. Geysers of ice and dust spouted and erupted from its sunlit surface like mini volcanoes, before being whipped away by the solar wind to join the tail. Jules had joined us.

'Wow, that's amazing,' was all he could say, 'Awesome!'

The second probe shot out, straight at the comet. It took a few minutes to find a landing site and start transmitting.

'Good data being received,' Dixie announced, giving a thumbs up. 'I'll tell the Captain and Astromin HQ that our mission was successful.'

We watched as the comet carried on its lonely journey, pulled by the Sun's gravity. As it flew closer to the Sun, it would warm up, become more active and the tail would brighten, maybe enough for people to see it on Earth. Then it would swing around the Sun and shoot away, back into the cold, dark depths of space.

Later that afternoon we were back in Dixie's office.

'Captain,' Dixie suddenly exclaimed. Her tone made me sit up, alert. The Captain spun his chair around, eyebrow raised. 'I can't find the key for the taser locker. I'm doing my weekly routines and it's gone. I've looked everywhere.'

'It's OK, Dixie, you've just put it down somewhere. You've been pretty distracted recently,' he added kindly. 'It'll turn up, I'm sure. Have you checked all your pockets?'

I could tell Dixie was upset and angry with herself. The locker, just above her desk, held our tasers and the spare magazines of cartridges, the two pronged 'bullets' that delivered the electric charge.   I thought I should help, so I started sniffing, under the desk, around the office and the rest of the flight deck. Nothing. We took another tour of the ship, this time with my nose to the ground, sniffing for clues. Eventually we gave up and went to see Mo.

Dixie explained the situation and asked Mo to print a new key. The 3D printer, down in the engineering workshop, was normally used to print spare parts.

'OK,' said Mo, 'This way.' She led us down the spiral staircase. There was a smell of warm electronics and the faint hum and buzz of a working spaceship. Mo tapped a few commands into the printer's computer. A picture of a key and a recipe for production appeared. She slotted two cartridges into the cartridge port, then clicked the start command. The printer began to hum quietly.

'It'll take a couple of minutes, Dixie, then it has to cool.'

Sure enough, ten minutes later, the key was safely stowed away in Dixie's hip pocket.

'I'm due a break,' declared Mo, 'Why don't we go and have a coffee in the lounge?'

'Sure,' replied Dixie, 'That'll be nice. I'll see you there. First, Izzie needs her dinner.'

My ears pricked up, fully alert. As a highly trained, specialist space dog, words like 'dinner', 'food' or 'treat' have this effect on me.

After I was fed, we joined the others in the lounge. Jules and Eva were there playing a game of chess. As we entered Eva turned around.

'Oh, hi, Dixie. Any news? Maybe we should switch on the news channel?'

'No, no news, thanks for asking, Eva.'

We spent the evening chilling with Mo and the others. That night I went to bed with a heavy heart. It would take several days for the ship from Vela to fully search the region of the explosion. I could hear Dixie was awake for some time. I knew she was concerned about Dan and bothered by the missing key. Eventually, she dozed off.

I woke to the melodious sound of Dixie's alarm clock playing its wake-up tune – the Star Wars theme. Dixie said the tune always encouraged her to jump out of bed and start a new day in space. We headed to the flight deck.

'G'morning, Captain.'

'Hi,' I woofed.

'Ah, Dixie, how did you sleep?' he asked, knowing the answer from the bags under Dixie's eyes and not waiting for an answer. 'No news from Vela yet, I'm afraid. The Space Rangers from Mars Orbiter are joining the search. They have better search capability. If any shuttles did get away, they'll find them.'

Dixie smiled wanly, 'Thanks, Captain. I know the rangers, and they know Dan. They'll work night and day to find him.'

Dixie was referring to our old friends, Captain Jack Turner and ranger Ramirez, who helped us save the Galileo Base from Sun Tzu's ghastly gang. Dixie knew there was nothing to be done but to put on a brave face and carry on as normal.

And it was a normal day, except for the fire...

It was late evening and many people had retired to their cabins when a loud and incessant warbling started up over the whole ship. 'Fire in the kitchen, fire in the kitchen,' the automated voice kept repeating. A fire on a spaceship is probably the most dangerous event that can happen, short of being smashed up by an inconsiderate, roaming asteroid.

Dixie flew for the door and ran to the kitchen, with me at her heels. T'unc had just arrived, in his pyjamas. He grabbed a fire extinguisher and started putting out a fire on a cooker. The ventilation system had automatically isolated itself and the air was heavy with carbon dioxide from the extinguisher. By the time the Captain and others had arrived, T'unc had the fire out. Thick smoke hung around the ceiling and swirled down the walls.

'What happened?' demanded the Captain, coughing.

T'unc looked crestfallen. 'There was a pan on the stove. It looks like something in it caught fire.' He paused, 'I don't understand it. I didn't leave it there.' He looked up at the assembled crew. 'Has anyone been using the kitchen?'

Everyone shook their head.

'All right,' concluded the Captain, 'It's late. We'll carry out an investigation and lessons learnt review first thing in the morning.'

'It's OK, T'unc,' said Smithy kindly, 'I'll help you clear up.'

'I'll help, too,' added Jules.

Next morning, Dixie's first task was to investigate the fire. How the pan had been left on the heat remained a mystery. Dixie was puzzled and, despite talking to everyone, could not understand what had happened.

'Someone's lying, Izzie,' she confided.

She decided to return to her office. As we headed past her desk, something shiny caught my eye. It was the missing key! I woofed and slid under the desk, grabbed it with my paw and dragged it out for Dixie to see.

Dixie looked down. 'The missing key! But we looked under there, didn't we? Strange.' She picked up the key and screwed up her face in thought. 'Maybe it was stuck behind the desk and fell down after we searched. Anyway...'

She opened the taser cabinet. Both guns were there, as were the four magazines of cartridges. She examined the guns, bent down and held them for me to sniff.

'This one's been used', I woofed. Dixie sniffed the gun.

'Hmmm,' she murmured, 'And this cartridge looks bent, as if it's been used and replaced in the magazine, but I can't be sure.'

Dixie returned the taser to its cabinet then locked it, putting the key in her drawer.

But that wasn't the only unsettling thing that happened that day.

Chapter 6 - Sabotage

That afternoon Dixie was completing her reports whilst eating a plate of custard creams. She threw me little bits, which I wolfed down in one gulp. She wasn't her normal self, but the colour had returned to her cheeks. There was still no news about Dan, one way or the other. Suddenly the intercom crackled into life.

'Captain, Mo here. You'd better come to the engine room. You need to see this.'

'Hi, Mo, what's up?'

'The rear ladar unit is damaged. You'd better come down, sir.'

The Captain span his chair to face us. Dixie and I were both peering around the cubicle, listening. He raised an eyebrow and gestured with a movement of his head.

'Come on.'

When we arrived, Mo was in discussion with Jules. She looked up.

'Thanks for coming down, Captain, come and look at this.'

Mo led them down the spiral staircase into the workshop. On a worktop, a piece of equipment about the size and shape of a bicycle pump lay under a camera.

'Look at this,' she repeated, pointing to the screen. It showed an x-ray image of the inner electronics of a ladar unit.

'What am I looking for, Mo?' the Captain asked.

'This is the damaged rear ladar unit. We need it so we can see approaching ships or asteroids. Without its laser beam, we are blind behind us. I can't fix this until I have a spare and they can only be obtained from Earth or Lunar Orbiter Alpha. These things are expensive, and they just don't fail.'

The Captain frowned. 'No spares on board? That's not good, but if these units don't fail what's gone wrong?'

'Look here,' Mo indicated a blackened region on the image before continuing, 'See the scorching? It looks like radiation damage, but I don't think it is. It's too large an area, there's too much damage. Of course, this is a new model so there could be a manufacturing fault, but there's a third possibility,' Mo looked the Captain in the eye and paused, 'This could have been done deliberately.'

The Captain raised his eyebrows. Dixie chipped in, 'Why do you say that, Mo?'

'The damage could have been done with a taser. Look at those two marks there and there,' she pointed at the image, 'The pattern looks like taser prongs. The voltage given by a taser would certainly do damage like this.' She turned to Dixie, 'You told me the key for the taser cabinet was missing, maybe someone has taken a gun?'

'I found the key this morning and none were missing. Although we did wonder if one had been fired recently. When did this damage occur?'

'I noticed it about 45 minutes ago,' replied Mo.

'So if the damage was done then, it should be easy to trace who was here and why? Anyway, the tasers were all locked up then,' replied Dixie.

'I wish it were that simple,' Mo countered. 'I've only just discovered the damage but there should have been an alarm when it failed. The alarm has been disabled. I've checked the computer log, and someone switched it off a week before launch. I reckon the ladar was tampered with in the last day or so. Someone has come in here and sabotaged it, and it was planned before we left.'

Jules caught my eye. He was looking pale and I noticed his heart rate was high. I could smell he was sweating. Dogs notice this sort of thing, especially highly trained, specialist space dogs. I couldn't say anything, but I was suspicious. Dixie turned to Jules.

'Jules, you were on night shift last night, were you here all night?'

'Sure,' Jules replied, hesitantly, 'Except for a meal with Eva and an hour or so on the flight deck. Oh, and of course, when we had the fire in the kitchen.'

'So, engineering could have been empty for what? Two hours?' We all looked at Jules.

'I guess so,' Jules shrugged.

'Right, I'm going to double check the taser cabinet.' Dixie announced, 'Then question everybody on the ship and check our files on all the passengers. Jules, send me a list of times you were away from engineering as best you can recall.'

Dixie turned and started to climb the stairs. 'Come on, Izzie, let's investigate.'

We went back to the flight deck. Dixie opened the taser cabinet. Both tasers were still there, showing a full charge. She took a small device from a drawer and scanned the area for fingerprints and DNA. When the results appeared, she shook her head.

'Nothing unusual.' Dixie indicated the desk, 'Up here, Izzie, have another sniff. Who's been here?'

I jumped onto Dixie's chair then up to the desk. I sniffed all around the desk and cabinet. There was an unusual smell. It wasn't strong and I couldn't place it. I gave my 'suspicious but not sure' bark. Dixie nodded.

'Not much more we can do here, Izzie, let's go and question the passengers.'

We questioned all six passengers and, without exception, they all claimed they had been in their cabins all night. Zolotov had retired to his cabin straight after dinner and said he was woken by the alarm. Joe, Baz and Jamie had stayed up until midnight watching an old 2D film and Jas and Françoise told us they left the passenger lounge at the same time, around ten.

We found the Captain to brief him. He frowned. 'I don't like this, Dixie. Maybe it was a manufacturing fault that put the ladar out of action. But if it was sabotage, who would do it and what would they be trying to achieve? In any case we need to be cautious and tighten security. Re-programme the locks on engineering, the flight deck and the crew quarters, then do that background check on the passengers and see what comes up. OK?'

'Right away, Captain,' responded Dixie. We went back to our cubicle and Dixie started the checks. As she called up files from the ship's computer, I sat on the desk watching. First up was Françoise, the IT and communications expert heading for Thisbe. Dixie reviewed her personal details, date of birth, official documentation, qualifications and history. Nothing sprang out as unusual, so she started to check the others. Jas, the Iranian born mining engineer and astrobiologist, also going to Thisbe. Jamie the chef, Asasiama, or Baz to most people, the Nigerian doctor, Joe the geologist and Yuri Zolotov the research scientist, all going to Mars Orbiter. There was some data missing but nothing seemed suspicious. All had photographs except Dr Zolotov.

Dixie paused, nibbling a biscuit. She absent-mindedly gave me a piece, then reached into her bottom drawer and removed two digi-cameras, each about the size of a shirt button.

'Old tech, Izzie, but I'll put one of these in each corridor. I'll connect them to the wi-fi so we can record any movement.'

A short while later both cameras were in place, barely noticeable. Dixie called up the pictures on her wristband.

'That should do it, Izzie. Come on, dinner time!'

I woofed happily. I had smelt chicken pie earlier. Yum! Delicious!

Later that evening I was hungry. Dixie had dozed off in the comfy chair in our cabin, so I thought I would wander down to the kitchen on the off chance I might find T'unc, Smithy or Jamie there. The light was on. I trotted round the cabinets but couldn't see anyone. However, I did notice the door to the walk-in fridge was open. I knew I'd find a nibble there, so in I went. I know I shouldn't have, but I was very peckish. As I was surveying the shelves, deciding what wouldn't be missed, a shadow flickered across the open door. I turned round and, to my horror, the door was closing. Before I could get there, the door had shut. Suddenly, it was cold and very dark. It reminded me of the time, in Dublin, when I had become lost and started my life as a stray. I barked and barked, then I started scrabbling at the door with my paws, but it was no good. It was metal and my paws just slipped off. I knew there was a door handle inside, but I couldn't reach it. Luckily, I had a fur coat, but my paws and my nose soon started to feel numb with cold. I barked some more. The noise echoed around the fridge. I started shivering, I had no idea of the time, or how long I had been trapped. I didn't think I could survive until the morning. The fridge was so cold. Little ice crystals started forming on my fur, turning it white. I curled up to save heat. Soon, I was getting too cold to bark.

Suddenly, the door opened and light and warm air flooded in.

'Izzie! What are you doing there?' exclaimed Dixie.

I tried to explain it wasn't by choice, but the whimpers hardly came out between the shivers. Dixie reached in and picked me up.

'You're like a block of ice!' Tell me about it, I thought. Dixie pulled a towel from a rail, wrapped me up tight and ran to the clinic. My breathing was quite shallow.

'Your pulse is weak, you're in stage two hypothermia. It's a good job I found you when I did!'

She rubbed my cold, damp fur with dry towels then wrapped me in a warm towel and a silver blanket. Using a large syringe, she gently dripped warm water in my mouth as I lay there. Slowly I started to warm up. My nose and legs were numb and, as I warmed up, they tingled painfully. After an hour, I felt better and sat up.

'Someone shut me in the fridge,' I woofed.

Dixie looked cross. 'Don't go near that fridge again. Hear me? Or you'll really be in the doghouse!' Then her face softened. 'Come on, let's get a snack, then it's bed. That's why I went to the fridge in the first place, to get a snack. Lucky for you I was hungry!'

Chapter 7 – Mars Orbiter

I woke to the Star Wars tune. I was feeling much better, although one paw was still a little sore. Dixie sat up, yawned and switched on the TV. After checking Orbit News Live (sadly, no news about Dan), she switched to a new channel. A view of Mars filled the screen, dull orange and red, sombre and silent against the star-spangled blackness of space. The south of the planet was in winter and water and carbon dioxide ice covered the South Pole. The centre of the screen was dominated by the huge, deep Hellas crater, home of the Galileo Base and last resting place of Dixie's parents. Given the memories, and with Dan still missing, Dixie was subdued.

'Look, Izzie, see those two glints of light? There.' She pointed at the screen. 'That's Phobos and Deimos, the two moons of Mars. They are named after the sons of the god Mars; the names translate as fear and terror.'

Now, I'm a plucky, brave sort of dog, but these names made my spine tingle, especially after what happened the last time we were on Mars. It turned out I was right to be concerned.

'I have a sense of déja vu,' said Dixie sombrely, 'Anyway, we'll be docking at Mars Orbiter around noon.'

Mars Orbiter was the huge supply station orbiting the planet. On the screen, it was just a speck gleaming in the soft sunlight, light that had left the Sun only minutes ago before flashing past us on its way to the outer Solar System and beyond.

Dixie took me to the gym. Smithy was there. To my embarrassment, Dixie told her about the fridge incident. Smithy looked concerned then chuckled. She loved to make everyone laugh, especially in tense situations.

'That'll teach you, Izzie. You were a lucky dog!' No sympathy there, then. She continued, 'Funny how the door shut on you, though, shouldn't have been anyone in the kitchen at that time of night. Now, have you heard this one?' she asked Dixie, between puffs from the rowing machine. Dixie looked up from the screen on the cross trainer, she was watching the latest news.

'Which one?' she asked, only half listening.

'Why can't dogs work the DVD remote?' asked Smithy, puffing as she pulled the rowing handle faster. Dixie thought about it and shook her head.

'Because they always hit the paws button!' she laughed, letting go of the rowing handle and stopping to catch her breath. 'Got that one from T'unc's nephew, Stevie. Here, what dog keeps the best time? Eh?' Dixie shook her head again. 'A watch dog!'

I raised my eyebrow and tilted my head. Dixie winked at me.

'What about a riddle, Dixie? What can't you see but travels along the ground following you everywhere?'

'Hmmm! Let me think?' Dixie went quiet for a while, looking at her feet as she increased speed on the cross trainer. Dixie looked up. 'Got it! The soles of my feet! Good one, Smithy.'

We soon completed our exercises and headed off for breakfast.

'Morning, T'unc,' called Dixie, as we entered the canteen.

'Morning, Dixie, nearly there,' he nodded towards the giant screen showing the red planet, slowly growing bigger. T'unc whispered conspiratorially to me.

'Bit of leftover chicken for you today, Izzie, even though you don't really deserve it after last night's escapade. Yes, I heard all about it.'

Overcoming my embarrassment, I woofed in appreciation and wagged my tail as we sat down. Dixie always sat in a corner, her back to the wall, watching the room. All six passengers were present. The three technicians, who were due to disembark at Mars Orbiter, were sitting together quietly talking and eating, the two women bound for Thisbe were enjoying a laugh on a nearby table and Dr Zolotov sat on his own, sipping coffee with his head in an old textbook. He was also disembarking for his onward journey to Titan, the moon of Saturn that provided so much of the Earth's methane gas, needed to make plastics. That was a lot further, another three months travel.

Once I had finished my food, which took about ten seconds, I wandered around the canteen, sniffing. As I passed Zolotov I could sense and smell he was anxious. To be fair, another three months travel followed by a year in the higher radiation levels around Titan might make anyone anxious. I stopped to look at him, he was checking his watch. Our eyes locked. He seemed surprised to see me. I saw a certain emptiness before he looked away, stood up and limped off.

'Come on, Izzie,' interrupted Dixie, 'No time for watching the world go by. We're needed on the flight deck.'

I turned to follow Dixie. We were decelerating quickly now so my feet felt a little unsteady. Once we arrived, I let Dixie deal with her pre-docking tasks. I lay in my basket with Ruff the squirrel sitting quietly beside me.

Around noon, the detail of Mars Orbiter was visible. The circular accommodation and workshop unit looked like a huge silver doughnut shining in space, speckled with little portholes of light. Arrays of solar cells rose above and below it like huge sails. There were four docks, giant lattices of aluminium that looked so fragile they could break off any minute. One dock contained another space barge that had been damaged by a small asteroid, judging by the football sized hole in one of its cargo containers. A very rare event and lucky escape for the crew. Modern ships were designed with a reactive elastic sealant in the hull that could expand and seal a hole less than the size of a tennis ball. Anything bigger would cause a rapid decompression. Slung underneath the station was a smaller dock for two Federal Space Rangers' ships.

Both were missing, taking part in the search for survivors from the Buzz Aldrin.

'Yuri Gagarin, this is Mars Orbiter, come in,' the speaker crackled.

'Mars Orbiter, this is Captain Jim Nokes of Yuri Gagarin. Request final docking approach.'

'That's confirmed, Captain. Dock four. Oh, and I hope you've remembered the chocolate digestives and marmite this time! My engineer is desperate, ran out two weeks ago.'

'Sure have,' replied the Captain, chuckling.

Dixie leant forward to the microphone. 'You can tell Jenny that the biscuits and a year's supply of marmite are safely stowed in container one.'

I knew Jenny. She was at the Space Academy when we were there. She was always fun to be with. She brought a jar of marmite to every meal and would put it on toast, sausages, chips, pizza, her finger for me to lick, anything. Only chocolate digestives were safe.

'OK, will do. Captain, the guidance system is locked on, we can bring her in from here.'

We watched as the dock approached and we glided round, our shadow falling over the space station. The structure grew larger and larger until it filled our screens. Finally, there was a slight jolt as the docking cradle engaged, grabbing the ship in its claw-like grip.

Dixie and I left to open the air lock to the passenger ramp. We had only just opened the outer door and locked the passenger ramp in place when the three technicians came ambling down the corridor carrying their bags.

Jamie was leading. 'Hey, Dixie, thanks for the trip. I enjoyed helping T'unc. Maybe we'll see you on the return trip in a few months.'

Dixie smiled. 'Look forward to it. The rest of your gear is in container one, which we'll be unloading shortly.'

The three technicians disappeared off down the corridor leading to Mars Orbiter's control room.

'Right, Izzie, we just need to disembark Dr Zolotov then we can offload the container.'

I could hear his limp before I could see him. He came around the corner from the passenger area, walking fast, bag over his shoulder. He nodded curtly as he passed. I had been sure he was going to be trouble, but I guess I was wrong, I thought. Zolotov turned at the bottom of the ramp and looked back. He smiled, a smile that made me feel uneasy, then he was gone. As we turned to go, a voice called us. Striding up the ramp was Jenny, Mars Orbiter's engineer.

'Dixie!' she called again. Dixie threw her arms around her and gave her a big hug.

'Jenny! It's lovely to see you!'

'And you, Dixie,' Jenny replied, then, looking down at me wagging my tail 'And of course you too, Izzie, you gorgeous little girl!'

'Hi,' I woofed happily, sniffing to see if she had any marmite on her finger. Jenny took Dixie's hand and her voice changed, serious and sad now.

'We heard about Dan's ship. I'm desperately sorry. You never know, he may have had time to escape….' Her voice tailed off.

'I know Jenny. We knew working in space could be dangerous. We knew the risks, but still we chose this career. Anyway, I haven't given up hope yet.' Dixie's voice trembled and her eyes glistened. She sniffed. Jenny, old friend that she was, changed tack.

'I wondered if I could help with your ladar problem. Do you want me to have a look?'

'Sure, why not? I'll take you to Mo in engineering then complete the offloading. She'll be pleased to see you.'

Chapter 8 – The Inspector

We left Jenny with Mo and went down to the cargo deck. Smithy was at the container docking computer. We had two cargo containers full of supplies slung underneath, one for Mars Orbiter and one for Thisbe.

Unloading was a simple process. A small, remotely controlled tug detached itself from Mars Orbiter. As it headed our way, its orange, cubical shape was highlighted against the background stars. Short bursts of gas vented to correct its course until it hovered next to the container. Clunk. Shiiiiiissssshhh. A quiet hiss and the computer confirmed that the container was disengaged.

'Mars Orbiter, you have control,' chimed Smithy.

We watched the container slowly move away from the ship. The tug skilfully turned it around, the sunlight catching it as it moved out of our shadow. In no time, the tug had the container lined up with Mars Orbiter's cargo dock. Four large clamps grabbed it and locked it in place.

'Container engaged and delivered, status green, thanks, Smithy!'

'No problem, Mars Orbiter, enjoy the goodies! Out.'

We would travel to Thisbe with just one container. Once there, we would leave it and load two from the mine, full of metals for Earth.

'Good job, Smithy,' congratulated Dixie, looking at the time on her wristband. 'We have time for a quick bite before our new passenger arrives. You going to join us?'

'Sure,' replied Smithy, 'I'll see you in a few minutes.'

We caught up with Mo and Jenny troubleshooting the ladar problem. They were discussing whether they could bypass the damaged unit's circuits, then use a spare circuit card from the launch engine once we were at full speed. We left them running a test and headed for the canteen. Smithy was already there. We had nearly finished our food when Mo and Jenny turned up. Mo shook her head.

'No joy, great idea of Jenny's but it didn't work.'

Jenny shrugged and sat down with her tray. 'Like Mo, I thought the damage looked suspicious. Could be a manufacturing fault but defects like that are very rare. When the Rangers return from the rescue mission, I'll raise it with them. Anyway,' she smiled, 'it's nice to catch up with you guys.'

They discussed the strange events that had been happening on the ship then caught up with general news. As Jenny stood up to leave, she squeezed Dixie's arm.

'I expect we'll hear some good news soon,' she said.

Dixie had a lump in her throat but managed to respond. 'Come on, I'll walk back with you. Our new passenger will be arriving soon.'

At the passenger ramp Jenny waved goodbye. 'See you on the return trip,' she called as she turned the corner with a final wave, nearly bumping into a tall, lean man. He walked purposefully along the corridor, stopping when he reached Dixie.

'Khalil Ali, your passenger,' he announced, 'And you are...?'

'Officer Symon, pleased to meet you. I'm here to register you on board.'

Ali looked down his hooked nose at Dixie, then turned to look at me. He gave me a distasteful look.

'A dog, hmmm. Well, Officer, I'm from Astromin and I'm here to do a spot inspection. I will be with you for a few days. You'd better let your Captain know.'

'Of course, Mr Ali.'

'Doc-tor Ali, if you please.'

'Of course, Dr Ali, but first there are some security checks we need to go through. Please step this way.'

Once the security checks were complete and Dr Ali had gone to locate his cabin, Dixie closed the door and called the Captain. We could hear him groan when he heard who had arrived.

'He has heard about the ladar unit, Captain, so expect him on the flight deck in a few minutes.'

'Thanks, Dixie, as if we don't have enough on our plate. Get back here then.'

Sure enough, Dr Ali was on the flight deck within ten minutes.

'Ah, Captain,' he started. 'Doc-tor Ali. I'm here to carry out a spot inspection. I hear you've had a problem with your ladar unit.'

The Captain stood up and held out his hand for Ali to shake. Ali ignored it and started to walk about the flight deck, looking at the screens.

'Yes, Doctor,' said the Captain, pointing to me, 'Dixie Symon, my security officer is investigating.'

Ali turned on his heel to face the Captain.

'Ah, yes, we met when I boarded. Any relation to the Symons of Mars fame?'

'Indeed, Doctor, their daughter,' replied the Captain.

'Well, that'll cut no ice with me,' sneered Ali. 'So, you have no idea what happened?'

'As I say, Doctor, my security officer is investigating,' the Captain replied firmly. 'Dixie, please update the good Doctor on the ladar situation.'

'Yes, sir. Doctor, please, come and have a seat,' Dixie replied, indicating the spare chair in her cubicle. Ali started to walk over.

'Right, but as soon as you have briefed me, I want to inspect all your passenger records, then go down to engineering to inspect their operating procedures and maintenance records.'

The Captain spoke up. 'We have twelve days to Thisbe, Doctor, you may as well take your time.'

'Oh, I will, Captain, I will,' Ali responded, 'But you should know I will be transferring to your sister ship the Space Barge Patrick Moore in three days, to return to Mars Orbiter.'

'No problem, I'll see to it,' replied the Captain. Now as you no doubt know, dogs, especially highly trained, specialist space dogs, have very good hearing so only I heard him mutter 'It'll be my pleasure'.

Doctor Ali spent the next two days picking over our records in great detail. However the Captain, with Mo and Dixie's help, ran a well managed ship. Ali couldn't find much wrong and, to the crew's amusement, he became more and more frustrated as the hours wore on. At least it passed the time and took our minds off Dan.

On the evening of the second day the Captain, Dixie and Mo assembled in the crew lounge after dinner to hear Dr Ali's report. He went through his findings but hadn't found many problems, and none of any importance, except one.

'My main concern, of course, is the ladar,' he explained. 'I've examined the damage and I think a manufacturing defect is very unlikely. In that case, it appears that someone on this ship stole a taser, entered engineering, which should be secure, and damaged the company's property. And we have no idea who might have done this. What do you say to that?'

Dixie spoke first. 'We know someone had access to two secure areas. It could have been anyone.'

'I don't believe it was one of the crew,' the Captain chipped in.

'I didn't say it was, Captain,' continued Dixie, 'We know the crew members well and they have all been security checked. What concerns me is that the alarm had been disabled by someone in Lunar orbit. That means they had been on the ship in dock. That points to an inside job, as does the fact that they had access to the door codes. This was well planned.'

'I agree,' added Mo, looking directly at Ali. 'You need to initiate an investigation with Astromin HQ. Four passengers left at Mars Orbiter; you need to have them investigated.'

'For all we know the person who did this is still on board.'

'That only leaves Jas or Françoise and the crew,' explained Mo, 'And anyway, why would someone go to that trouble and risk staying on board?'

'There can only be one reason,' the Captain growled. 'By damaging the ladar, someone wants to approach unnoticed. But why?'

They carried on discussing the issue for a while. Finally, it ended when Doctor Ali promised to investigate further once he arrived back at Mars Orbiter. Even so, as they stood up to leave, it was clear that everyone had some unresolved concerns about the situation.

I watched Dr Ali leave the room. Can we trust him, I thought? There were too many people coming and going for my liking.

Chapter 9 –Thisbe Metal Mine

The next morning, after a course adjustment, we were ready to dock with the Space Barge Patrick Moore, and transfer Dr Ali for his return to Mars Orbiter. Docking at speed, and I mean 600,000 kilometres per hour, was often done but, even so, it was not routine and could be dangerous. The atmosphere on the flight deck was tense. Eva was at the controls. The main screen showed the Patrick Moore flying steadily alongside. It was hard to imagine we were traveling so fast yet were only 1000 metres from each other.

The captain of the Patrick Moore appeared on a screen. After a few greetings and pleasantries, he came down to business.

'Jim, how do you want to play this?'

I knew our Captain would want Eva in control. It was essential to be ready to take the manoeuvre to manual if needed, and Eva was one of the best pilots in the fleet. One false move and we would have two damaged spaceships, wrecks even.

'Let us bring her over to you, Gerry,' replied our Captain.

'Roger that, Jim, you have control on your command.'

The Captain turned to Eva. 'All yours, Eva. I'll watch the proximity sensor.'

'Thanks, Captain, here we go.'

We started to creep towards the other ship. Slowly it loomed larger and larger in the screen. We could see people nervously watching us through its windows.

The artificial intelligence computer, monitored by Eva, was controlling the ship with laser like precision. The room was holding its breath as we crept closer. Suddenly, there was a slight shudder that made me jump.

'Magnetic lock engaged. Clamp engaged. Well done, Eva.'

The room relaxed. I watched the airlock open and Doctor Ali cross over into the other ship. 'And good riddance,' the Captain announced to all on the flight deck.

'Woof,' I agreed.

A man with grey hair approached from the other ship and handed a package to Dixie. It was Gerry, their Captain. Alongside him trotted Alfie the Alsatian, my classmate at the Academy. I woofed in greeting but he couldn't hear me. Gerry and Dixie shook hands and held a brief conversation. Dixie patted Alfie on the head and let him lick her hand. After a few words, the airlock was closed.

The Captain pushed the disengage button on the screen and the two ships started to drift apart.

'All clear, Gerry, you go below us then we'll turn.'

'OK, Jim. By the way, I gave Dixie a little something for you. See you again, soon.'

'Thanks, Gerry, much appreciated, though I think you have the worst of the swap.'

Gerry chuckled, 'I've met Dr Ali before. All in the line of duty, eh? Anyway, all the best, bye.'

The Captain waved and the screen went blank. All eyes turned to the other screen as we watched the Patrick Moore slowly sink below us and resume its course to Mars. A few minutes later we resumed our own course. Just then Dixie reappeared.

'Alfie says hi, Izzie, and here's the package for you, Captain.' Dixie handed over the package. The Captain pulled out a box of chocolates.

'Ah, salted caramels, my favourite. We'll put them in the canteen for this evening. Good old Gerry. Remind me to repay the favour. Dixie.'

'Yes, Captain.'

The trip to the Thisbe asteroid mine would take several more days. With Doctor Ali out of the picture, the crew returned to their routines. We had no reason not to trust each other but we kept a close eye on the remaining passengers, Jas and Françoise. Dixie regularly checked her minicams in the corridor for any unusual movement. The Captain maintained contact with the ship from Vela, which had reached the explosion site. Due to the amount of debris and minor asteroids, their sensors hadn't detected any escape shuttles. However, they planned to stay in the area and plot the courses of all these objects to confirm which were asteroids, which were debris and which, if any, were shuttles. In the meantime, they would pick up the ship's black box, which was still sending out a signal. They promised to keep in touch provided the expected solar storm didn't disrupt communications.

Every so often the Sun releases extra radiation from huge flare ups on its surface. These flares - or 'coronal mass ejections' - surf through the solar system at huge speeds, disrupting communications and raising background radiation to dangerous levels. Satellites around Earth, watching for these flares, had issued an alert a day earlier. The Earth was protected by its magnetic field, but we knew that tomorrow we would probably lose all communication and it could last three or four days or more.

Sure enough, within hours, we found we couldn't raise anyone on the radio. It was a communications blackout. We resigned ourselves to having no news until we arrived at Thisbe at the earliest.

The rest of the trip went without further problems. As we started decelerating, the Captain announced we would be arriving at Thisbe in a few hours. The screens displayed a black, deep space background, speckled with red, yellow and blue stars, Nearer, we could see Jupiter, small, distant and partially lit by the sun so it formed a crescent. Its four large moons shone as small dots of light as they orbited the gas giant.

Thisbe soon came into view. It looked like a huge potato as it spun slowly in the weak sunlight. It was old, very old. It had been created at the same time as the Solar System, unused and left over from the formation of the Earth and other planets, four and a half billion years ago. Since then, it had orbited the Sun in the Asteroid Belt, cold, gloomy and lonely, thousands of kilometres from its nearest neighbour. That is, until the mine arrived.

The lights from the mine accommodation and control centre were visible near the top, or what on Earth would have been the North Pole. Nearby, dimly lit, was the processing plant that increased the purity of the ore before transport to Earth. We could see the huge mine transporters crawling on the surface like ants, scurrying between the plant and the mine workings. The scars from the mining could be seen running south, shining as the freshly exposed ore caught the sunlight. Once in orbit around the asteroid, we would send down our container of supplies, unload the cargo deck and, finally, bring up two full cargo containers for Earth.

A voice came over the speaker against a background of hissing, fading in and out a little. Radiation levels from the solar storm were still higher than normal, causing some disruption to communications, but we could hear well enough.

'Yuri Gagarin, you are clear to enter orbit. We'll send a shuttle for your passengers. We also have three heading back to Earth. Some good news, the ship from Vela picked up an escape shuttle two days ago. We think it must have been from the Buzz Aldrin, but it was scorched beyond recognition. The guy inside was in a pretty bad way. He's still in our sickbay, can't remember much, but he's stable. I know you have a relative of one of the crew on board, maybe they can come down and identify this guy? Let's hope it's good news.'

As soon as we heard this, Dixie and I raced over to the flight deck console. The Captain looked up at her and smiled before replying.

'Confirm that, Thisbe. Dixie, our scientific and security officer, had her brother on board the Buzz Aldrin. She can come down as soon as we've off-loaded our cargo.'

The Captain switched off the comms. 'Fingers crossed, Dixie. We'll get you down there ASAP.'

'Thanks, Captain,' was all Dixie could say. I could see she was a little bit choked up, but she soon recovered herself. 'I'll get ready.'

Chapter 10 –Open and Shut Case?

It wasn't long before we were in orbit above Thisbe. The asteroid had no atmosphere so the lights of the mine could be clearly seen below, crisp and sharp. The mining machines moved slowly up and down, closer now, looking more like giant beetles than ants, scurrying to dump their loads in the processing plant hoppers. A thin cloud of dust rose from the hoppers and drifted off into space, its progress undisturbed by Thisbe's weak gravity and lack of atmosphere. The dust formed a tail of fine particles in Thisbe's orbit, shining faintly in the weak sunshine.

As I was admiring this view, Dixie stood up impatiently. 'Come on, let's go and find Smithy to offload container two,' she called as she hurried away.

Our container was offloaded the same way as at Mars Orbiter. A space tug, sent up from the mine, latched onto the container and gently glided down to the mine cargo bay. As we returned to the flight deck it was alive with chatter as the Captain, Eva and Mo prepared the ship for the return trip. The Captain turned to Dixie.

'Ah, Dixie, the shuttle for you and our passengers will be arriving in about ten minutes. Is everything ready?'

'Yes, Captain, I'll just finish the paperwork,' replied Dixie, sitting down at her desk. Dixie had just completed the papers when the Captain called out again.

'Dixie!'

Dixie finished squaring off the digital papers on her nano-desk and brushed away a crumb. She was trying to hide her excitement about seeing Dan, if it was Dan down on Thisbe. She had a feeling. She poked her head around her cubicle door.

'Yes, Captain?' she replied, more calmly than she felt.

'We have an alert about an escaped prisoner. It turns out the guy from the escape shuttle was under arrest. He was being held in the mine's clinic but has gone missing.'

I noticed Dixie's heart skip a beat. 'Under arrest? I'll look at the alert. He can't go far, can he?'

Dixie switched on her wristband and punched a few buttons to bring up the alert. She froze, then drew her breath. Her chest tightened. She flicked the alert onto her desk screen. It opened full size. Looking at us was a face that reflected hers.

'What the....?' she muttered. She put her hand to her temple. She looked disorientated and dizzy. I stood up and put my paws on Dixie's knee so I could see better. The screen showed a picture of Dan! He must have survived! I looked at Dixie and wagged my tail and woofed excitedly. Dixie put her fingers to her lips. Recovering herself, she stuck her head around the partition.

'It's OK, Cap, I'll deal with this myself. Better put a hold on the new passenger transfer until I'm back.'

Dixie returned her gaze to the face on her screen. Thoughts and questions tumbled through my mind. Whoa, I said to myself, one at a time. I caught a couple in mid-flight - what was Dan doing under arrest and could he really be alive? Could he have survived the explosion of the Buzz Aldrin, after all? I felt a surge of hope. It is him. It must be. If it is, we'll find him, I thought.

Dixie buckled on her utility belt, smoothed down her clothes and punched the door button. As Dixie left the flight deck the Captain turned to his screen and looked at Dan's picture. He had never met Dan.

'That face looks familiar,' I heard him mutter.

Dixie strode down the corridor with me at her side. Her face was set and purposeful and her steps quick. I knew that look; she was focussed. She was on a mission.

Our passengers, Jas and Françoise, were waiting for us at the air lock. The shuttle soon arrived, and we took our seats. It was a short flight down to Thisbe. As the lights of the mine grew more distinct, I could feel Dixie's heartbeat increase. As soon as we docked, Dixie jogged down the ramp into Thisbe's Control Room. The room was large and dimly lit, mainly by the screens on the wall showing mining operations, geological strata, graphs and all sorts of other things you need to know to manage an asteroid mine. The entire front wall was a window overlooking the processing plant. The huge mine transporters could be seen trundling up to the feed hoppers and disgorging their dusty cargo of raw ore. A man stood next to a seated woman, discussing data on a screen. The woman was sitting at a U-shaped console, typing on a keyboard, her eyes moving between two screens. An alarm started beeping before being silenced.

'Officer Dixie Symon reporting, sir,' Dixie announced.

'Space Dog Izzie reporting,' I woofed, not wanting to be outdone.

'Officer Symon,' the man turned, his crooked smile offsetting his bright blue eyes and mop of sandy coloured hair. 'A pleasure to meet you and, er, your dog. I knew your parents. I'm Jim Cochrane, the mine manager here. I assume you're the crew member who might be related to our mysterious guest?' He raised an eyebrow.

'Yes, sir, I saw the alert about the escaped prisoner and thought I should report to you to see how I could help.' I woofed. 'Oh, and this is Izzie.'

The mine manager's smile became bigger and more crooked. Dixie noticed that the reason for this was a large scar on his left cheek.

'Jo, my engineer,' he pointed to the woman at the console, who smiled, 'Nice to meet you, Officer, Izzie.'

Dixie smiled and I wagged my tail.

'You've seen the alert?' asked the manager, looking Dixie straight in the eye.

'Yes, sir. He is my brother,' Dixie held his gaze.

'Well, that's some good news.'

'Thank you, sir. What's he done?' enquired Dixie.

'He's stolen a new and very secret electronic control board for our latest mining machine and copied the software to control it. It contains details about the new bio-mining operation, the type of ore eating bacteria we use, the conditions we keep them at, all very secret. We have questioned him, but he won't admit it and now we can't find him or it anywhere. We can't let him off this station with our secrets. Can I take it I have your full co-operation even though he is your brother?'

'Of course, sir, without question. I want to get to the bottom of this as much as you,' Dixie reassured him, 'I've ordered a lock down of our ship. But what makes you think it was him?'

'Look here,' he said, pointing to a screen.

Jo touched the screen and a video recording appeared. It showed a small, dimly lit room with a single desk, chair and screen in the centre. A door opened, streaming light into the room. A man entered, backlit from the corridor. He moved swiftly to the desk, his face in shadow. He reached under the desk, unscrewed a panel and pulled out a small electronic card, putting it into his jacket pocket. Then he plugged a wi-fi stick into a port, typed a few commands into the computer and waited for some data to download.

Dixie spoke. 'You can't see who that is.'

'Wait,' replied the mine manager. The figure removed the stick and turned to leave. As he did so the light lit up his face. It was Dan! The video continued as Dan left. The door closed, leaving the room dimly lit.

'Open and shut case, as they say, Dixie.'

Chapter 11 – The Missing Man

I realised there was something strange about the video. I couldn't figure out what but, in any case, this wasn't the Dan I knew. I could see Dixie was thinking the same.

'What do you think D...,' Dixie paused to stop herself from saying Dan, 'What do you think the prisoner's motive was for stealing the card and software?'

'That's the puzzling thing. He shouldn't even be here,' answered the manager. 'One of the ships from Vela found him in an escape shuttle a couple of days ago and brought him here. We were the closest medical help. We assume it was a shuttle from the Buzz Aldrin, but it was so badly scorched and damaged there were no markings, nor did he have any identification on him. When he was found, he was in a bad way, near death, almost frozen. The life support system was barely functioning. He's lucky to be alive. He can't remember much, not even his name. but our medic thinks that will come back soon. Anyway, his recovery is remarkable, and he's been in our sickbay since, well, before this. In fact, he was back there when we arrested him. He denies it of course, but we've shown him the video.'

Dixie responded. 'May I have a copy of the video and go and see the crime scene? Then we'll search for the prisoner.'

'Of course. Jo, send Dixie the video.'

'Already done, sir. Come on, Dixie, I'll take you downstairs to the room,' said Jo, standing up and leading the way. Once there, she ushered us in. Dixie went straight to the desk.

'Who would use this room?'

'Usually me or Brett, the mining engineer.'

'I'll need a list of people here at the mine. How many would there be?'

'We normally have 20 including six technicians who work outside with the machines. Right now, we have three extra, a research scientist and the two new crew members you brought with you. They are replacing me and Brett, as we're going back to Earth with you.'

'OK, u-huh,' said Dixie, thoughtfully. 'I'll check for prints and DNA. Has anyone done that yet?'

'No,' replied Jo, 'We don't have the gear.'

Dixie pulled a small device from her belt and scanned the keyboard. There were no fingerprints showing. They had been wiped, or the criminal had used some chemical substance to mask them, may be a silicone gel, an old trick. The DNA was more useful, three distinct strands showing up.

'Do you have the DNA prints of everyone on the mine, Jo?'

'Sure, we should have, we can look upstairs. Anything else?'

Dixie looked at me and raised an eyebrow. I had been sniffing around for scents and other clues. I wagged my tail.

'That should be all for now. Where are the video files stored?'

'I can show you that upstairs as well.'

Back in the control room, Jo ushered Dixie into a chair then sat down next to her. She called up the video files on the screen.

'That's strange,' announced Jo, 'I didn't notice before, but the file timestamp is later than when it was recorded.'

'Hmm, so someone might have tampered with it.'

Jo pulled up another screen. 'Pretty much everyone was logged in at the time, here, I'll send you the list. And I'll send the DNA prints too.'

Dixie's wristband vibrated as the files arrived.

'The DNA matches these three people, all of whom are allowed access to that room. There's me, Brett the mining engineer, and Jim, the mine manager. Nothing suspicious there.'

'So, if your new visitor stole the card and software, he left no DNA or fingerprints behind,' mused Dixie, 'Yet he didn't appear to be wearing gloves in the video. Still, it's possible. But then why tamper with the video, unless of course someone has edited it to hide some evidence.'

Dixie looked at her wristband and called up a file. 'There's another passenger on my list, an Alina.'

'She's the research scientist, she's only been here a month.'

'I suggest Izzie and I start the search of the building. We can stop by the clinic first.'

'The clinic is downstairs too,' explained Jo, leading the way.

The clinic was a large room with three beds, two neatly made, the other with its sheets thrown back. We looked into the other rooms; an office, bathroom, operating theatre and storeroom but there was no sign of anyone. Dixie spoke.

'Da... The prisoner was in here?' Dixie and I looked at each other. Jo nodded.

'We'll start a search,' Dixie volunteered.

'Woof,' I agreed. Dixie held the sheets on the unmade bed to my nose so I could follow the scent.

We started to search the building. Jo helped by unlocking doors and explaining to the crew what was happening. The base was about the size of a small luxury hotel designed for 30 people. Our final stop was a small maintenance workshop and store. The scent from the bedsheets was strong here. I alerted Dixie, who nodded to say she understood.

Jo explained. 'This is the emergency room and equipment store. We could stay here for four weeks if we had to. We have another one a kilometre away. On the wall we have 48-hour survival suits, and the cupboards are full of supplies, extra rations and so on. If the mine buildings were badly damaged, we could wait here for rescue or evacuate to the other location.'

'Could the prisoner have escaped to the off-site emergency room? Maybe we should check there?' asked Dixie.

'No, the door is alarmed. It would alert us if anyone entered, and we haven't seen that.'

We had a good look around and found nothing unusual, although I did wonder if I was the only one who noticed a survival suit was missing.

It had taken a couple of hours to complete the search. We hadn't found Dan, nor had I smelt any sign of the missing electronic card, so it must have been well hidden. We went back to the control room to report to the mine manager.

'The prisoner will turn up. He can't go far. The important thing is to ensure the card doesn't leave the mine,' explained Jim, 'So a search of anything leaving the asteroid is essential. Everything must be scanned before it goes on board your ship, including the passengers' personal luggage. Anyway, you must be hungry, Jo will sort some lunch for you. Thanks for your help.'

On our way to lunch, Jo explained about the mine. Apparently, Thisbe is a M-type asteroid, which means it is rich in metals, in fact about 50% metal, the rest being rock and ice. It is the thirteenth largest object in the asteroid belt and has a diameter of 225 kilometres. It spins so fast, its day is just six hours long, which is why the mine was built on the North Pole, so it could be in permanent sunlight. Thisbe orbits the Sun every 4.6 years.

After a meal of chicken and chips we took the mine's shuttle back to our ship. I knew Dixie was worried about Dan. She told me. People tell their pets all sorts of things and Dixie was no exception. There was no sign of Dan and I could see Dixie was on edge.

'Don't worry,' I woofed, 'He can take care of himself.'

'I just don't understand how Dan can disappear,' Dixie grimaced. 'We searched the whole base.'

Later, a tug brought the first cargo container of refined metal up to us. This was a tricky operation as any wrong move could severely damage our ship or even send it spinning into space. Thanks to some skilful manoeuvring the container was soon in place, slung directly below the ship.

I recalled the pre-flight seminar I had attended with Dixie. The cargo was made up of rare metals, the so-called technology metals that were in short supply on Earth, which explains why we had to go all the way to asteroids like Thisbe to mine them. Modern electronics needed these metals. A smartphone needs 62 different metals, including dysprosium which has unique magnetic properties. Asteroids provide a rich source of these metals. Some countries in Asia had these metals as natural resources they could mine, but they were scarce and very expensive to buy in Europe or America. This itself made asteroid mining worthwhile.

The second container was sent up. It was full of refined metal and some waste, mainly old equipment and packaging being sent back to Earth for recycling. By the time we had finished it was late afternoon.

Chapter 12 – Missing Motherboard

It wasn't long before the passengers, Brett and Jo, the two crew members returning home, and Alina, the research scientist, arrived by shuttle. Dixie, Smithy and I were ready to meet them. Alina was first. I noticed her striking sapphire blue eyes, they seemed to rove everywhere, taking in everything. Brett came next. He seemed a laid-back sort of guy, with blond hair down to his shoulders and grey eyes.

'Hey, man, I love space travel, just like Star Trek. I love Star Trek. Can I visit the flight deck later?'

'Sorry, sir,' replied Smithy firmly, 'The flight deck is strictly off limits to passengers.'

'Oh, well, we'll see,' he replied, smirking.

Jo was the last in the queue of three. She presented her backpack without a word, just smiling at Dixie.

We scanned their belongings without any sign of the stolen data card.

'OK, Dixie, lock the door,' the Captain ordered. 'I've spoken to Jim and he expects the prisoner and the card will turn up soon. We've alerted the Rangers. We have a schedule to keep and we're already running late.'

'Ay ay, Captain,' Dixie responded with a heavy heart. She had been hoping to see Dan but now she would have to leave him behind.

'Tell the Captain your concerns,' I woofed.

'You know Izzie, none of this makes any sense. I know Dan's innocent. I'm sure the video was tampered with. I'll talk to the Captain once we're on our way.'

With our cargo and passengers loaded, we left Thisbe. In addition to the mystery of the broken ladar, we now had the mystery of Dan's whereabouts. They say bad things come in threes. It wasn't long before the next strange thing happened.

I was up early and sitting in the flight deck next to Eva, waiting for T'unc to open the kitchen. Eva had been in command of the ship and was puzzled about an overnight alarm. She explained her concerns when the Captain arrived to take over.

'Morning, Eva, everything under control?' he asked, as he always did when he first arrived on the flight deck.

'Yes, more or less, Captain.' She paused, 'One strange alarm overnight. That cargo deck airlock seems to be playing up again. The alarm showed it open around 0200 hours for a few minutes, then it went back to normal. The strange thing was, well, the pressure indicator looks like it really did open.'

'I'll ask Dixie and Smithy to check it out. Thanks, Eva, I'll take over, you head off now.'

'Ay, Captain, see you later,' replied Eva as she stood up and stretched.

I accompanied Eva to the canteen. Dixie was already there, finishing her cereal and yoghurt. I had my usual biscuits. It wasn't long before the Captain called and asked Dixie to check out the cargo airlock.

'Come on, Izzie,' she gestured, 'We have a job to do.'

We found Smithy, who ran a diagnostic check on the door programme then tested the wiring. She shook her head.

'The lock is working fine but it does look as if the lock's programme was compromised last night. There are only two explanations. One, space radiation temporarily upset the system until it reset itself or two, and I know this sounds silly, the wiring was short circuited from outside the ship.'

Dixie frowned. 'You mean someone, or something, outside the ship manually shorted the wires so the air lock would open?'

'Uh-huh, crazy I know. It must have been the radiation.'

'This lock has been playing up all voyage, maybe we've missed something.'

'Maybe,' conceded Smithy doubtfully, returning her gaze to the monitor showing the diagnostics, 'I'll double check.'

'Thanks, Smithy.'

Next morning, I was up as soon as the Star Wars alarm went. I went straight to see if T'unc was in the kitchen, hoping to have an early breakfast. Sure enough he was. He was busy looking for something, muttering to himself. I trotted up to him and sat down, head to one side, wagging my tail, which is doggy code for 'is it food time yet?' He soon spotted me.

'Izzie, have you eaten the pie I left to cool on the worktop overnight, it's gone!' he quizzed me sternly before adding, 'And I'm sure some bottles of high vitamin juice have gone too. No, it can't have been you or there would be crumbs all over the place. So, who has taken them? I shall have words with the passengers and crew at breakfast.'

'I'm happy to investigate and if I find the pie can I eat it?' I woofed hopefully. T'unc didn't reply. I was still hungry, so gave him the doggy eyes look. It worked.

'Well, you may as well have your breakfast as you're here,' said T'unc resignedly, fetching my bowl and filling it with dog biscuits and a topping of ham bits.

I think I noticed it first. I sat up, alert, Dixie looked down from her desk, custard cream poised in mid-air.
'What is it, Izzie?'

'The ion drive hum has stopped,' I barked. This hum was barely noticeable to humans, but we dogs could hear it, though we tended to block it out, a bit like traffic noise at home. It didn't bother us, at least not me, a highly trained, specialist space dog.

Dixie tilted her head to one side, listening. 'That's odd, the engine hum has stopped.'

'Wuf,' exactly.

'Captain,' called Dixie, 'Have you noticed the change in noise. It sounds like the ion drive has stopped.'

Before the Captain could respond, an alarm sounded and a display of the ion drive appeared on the wall screen, flashing red in alarm mode.

Mo started interrogating the screens. 'I'm on it. I've started running a full diagnostic. So far power source looks normal, propellant management system looks …. er …. normal ………… power processing train …………. reads normal. Ion thruster all good too. That just leaves the control computer. Give me a few minutes.'

The ion drive was our engine that allowed us to travel at 600,000 kilometres per hour. In space there is no air resistance so we could maintain that speed without the drive. However, without the drive we could lose electrical power, we couldn't slow down and there would be no magnetic field around the ship to protect us from space radiation. Out here, in the asteroid belt, the radiation levels were deadly, and our health would be affected in days.

The Captain and Mo sped down to engineering to find out what was happening. Dixie continued her work, but she clearly wasn't concentrating.

'Come on, Izzie. I can't just sit here.'

We trotted off to the engineering control room. As we entered, we saw the Captain standing next to Mo. Jules was taking notes from the wall screens. The mood was tense.

'You're sure, Mo?' the Captain asked.

'There is no doubt about it, Captain. The motherboard has failed. The drive continued to operate normally until we reached full speed and the computer accessed the motherboard for the cruising speed programme, that's when it failed. I don't understand how this could happen.'

'OK, first things first then, use the spare to fix it then we'll find out who did this,' replied the Captain.

'That's the other crazy thing, sir,' muttered Mo meekly, her head down, 'The spare is missing.'

The silence in the room shouted WE'RE IN TROUBLE.

Chapter 13 – The Search is On

Eventually Dixie spoke up. 'When you say missing, Mo, do you mean it's not in the right place, but we'll find it if we look, or do you mean we don't appear to have a spare at all?'

'I'm sure I confirmed we had a spare before launch. It's been taken.'

My heart sank for Mo. I knew she was meticulous and would have followed all the pre-flight protocols and procedures. The records would show she checked the spare was there, but I sensed she was beginning to doubt herself.

'This is getting really serious,' commented the Captain before continuing. 'Without the ion drive we can't slow down. We can't get a replacement until we reach Mars. They'll have to fly one out to us so we can slow down to enter orbit. And the magnetic shield protecting us won't work, so we will be exposed to harmful doses of radiation.'

Maybe we'll all have to wear our space suits, I thought. That would be awkward.

Jules was still looking at the wall screens. I sidled up to him. There was something not right, his heart was racing and he was sweating, just like before when we found a problem with the ladar unit. Maybe he was just anxious, but my doggy intuition told me it was strange.

The Captain gestured. 'Dixie, hand out the anti-radiation tablets, then you and Izzie start a search of the ship to see if the missing motherboard can be found. I don't like what's been happening. First the ladar unit and the gun locker key, then the fire, the cargo air lock door and now this.'

'Don't forget about me being locked in the fridge and the missing food,' I chipped in.

'And then there's the missing food,' he added. Oh, I thought, no-one's told him about the fridge incident.

'We've had a complete change of passengers,' Dixie explained, 'So it's unlikely to be one of them, unless two are involved. There's the crew but..........' Her voice tailed off as she looked at the Captain.

'What about the prisoner from Thisbe? Could he be on board?' queried the Captain.

Dixie's face reddened. 'I...... I don't see how, sir. Smithy was watching the loading bay the whole time and Izzie and I checked the entire ship and didn't find anything unusual.'

The Captain looked Dixie in the eye. 'Well, we need to get on top of this, Dixie. Increase your patrols and investigate this damage,' commanded the Captain. He turned to Mo. 'Mo, keep this room locked. No-one is allowed in unless you or Dixie are here. I will update Astromin HQ and order a new motherboard.'

As all this unfolded, I was still observing Jules. His body language, scent and other clues made me suspicious. I was going to watch him more closely. The Captain headed for the door then turned back.

'When I find out who has done this, I'm going to eject them into space without a space suit!'

'I'm not sure that's allowed,' replied Dixie earnestly.

'Just get on with your job, Dixie,' the Captain snapped, 'and stop any more of these events happening.'

'Yes, Sir,' Dixie responded quietly. I walked over to sit next to Dixie and rub her leg. 'Never mind,' I woofed, 'His bark's worse than his bite!'

'And take that dog with you!' he barked as he disappeared around the corner and the door slid shut behind him.

'Never mind, Dixie,' Mo gave Dixie a comforting smile, 'Maybe you had better issue those anti-radiation tablets.'

'Good idea, Mo. Then I need to think, we need to work through this problem, but first let Izzie sniff that motherboard for clues.'

Mo held the motherboard for me to sniff. I could smell metal, burnt metal, and some human scent. The smell of burnt metal was strong and made it difficult to distinguish the other scents. I concentrated. I knew how important this was. There was Mo's scent and two more, I thought. Jules, definitely, and one other that smelt familiar but I couldn't place.

'OK, Izzie, done?' asked Dixie. I woofed yes.

'Right, come on, let's go and fetch those anti-radiation tablets. They're in the clinic.'

When we arrived, Dixie went straight to a large cupboard. The door slid open revealing shelves of medical supplies, medicines, all sorts, enough for a small hospital, which is exactly what the clinic was. Dixie reached up to the top shelf and paused.

'I don't believe it, Izzie, there are only a few boxes of anti-radiation tablets here, most are missing.'

Dixie rooted around some more. After a minute she stood back and shook her head.

'They were definitely here before launch, I checked everything. Someone has stolen them!'

I knew from her expression that this was not good, to say the least. Dixie stared at the empty space where the anti-radiation tablets should have been.

'It looks like we still have a few days' supply, I'll hand these out. The Captain will go spare!'

Sure enough, when we told the Captain, his face started to go red and he looked like he might explode. He opened his mouth to say something, then shut it again. He sat down and stroked his beard. I could feel him calming down.

'It'll be eight or nine days before we can meet a ship from Mars and repair the ion drive. We have enough tablets for a minimum dose until then and, if we conserve power, we have enough battery power to switch on the shields for a few hours in case there is a solar flare. But, Dixie, this has gone far enough, Astromin HQ need a rocket! They've been too slow and sloppy. Tell them to do a complete background check on all the passengers and crew. Then you'd better carry out a complete sweep of the ship for the missing motherboard.'

'Consider it done, Captain,' replied Dixie heading back to her desk to send a strongly worded message to Astromin HQ. She told them to do a full background report on all the crew and recent passengers and she wanted it now! Having said that, it would take at least five minutes for the signal to arrive at Earth and then another five minutes to return once they had an answer. Dixie stood up.

'Oh, just remembered!' Dixie muttered, 'I can check the digicams in the corridors.'

She called up the motion sensitive recordings and fast forwarded through the last two days. She frowned.

'Nothing, there's nothing unusual ...except the time seems to have frozen for an hour last night.'

'Hacked?' I suggested.

'You know, Izzie, I think the digicams were compromised in some way. But at least that gives us a timeframe for the crime. Come on, we're going investigating. We'll hand out the anti-radiation tablets at the same time.'

Great. Operation 'sniff and search' had begun, and I could keep an eye out for Jules as well. It's almost as good as hunting. I ran to her side and we headed for the passenger quarters. The first passenger cabin belonged to the woman with the sapphire blue eyes. The door opened almost as soon as Dixie buzzed. The woman was immaculately dressed in a pale blue shawar kameez suit.

'May I come in for a moment, I'm Officer Symon, it's Alina isn't it?'

Alina nodded and stood to one side. 'Sure, but what can I do for you, officer?'

Dixie explained that there was a temporary problem with the radiation shield and handed over a packet of tablets. Alina listened attentively, her blue eyes studying Dixie then, as I started sniffing around the room, she turned to watch me.

'That's unusual,' she quipped, turning back to Dixie, 'I mean for an ion drive to fail. What was the cause?'

'I didn't say the ion drive had failed. How do you know that?' Dixie asked, a little aggressively.

'The hum has stopped,' replied Alina, surprised by the question. 'Any idea why?'

'We're not sure, we're investigating,' replied Dixie guardedly, still watching me sniff around.

'Was it the motherboard?' asked Alina. Dixie turned back to Alina.

'What makes you think it was the motherboard?'

'Just guessing, but you have a spare, right? All ships carry a spare, it's a critical piece of equipment.' Alina read Dixie's expression and continued. 'I have heard of this before, a failed motherboard and a missing spare. It's the easiest way to disable a ship like this.'

'You seem to know a lot about it,' replied Dixie, becoming suspicious.

'I'm a research engineer, I'm take note of these things,' Alina retorted, perhaps a little too quickly.

I completed my sweep and sat next to Dixie. She looked down at me. I wagged my tail to say all clear. Dixie turned to leave.

'I can't discuss the investigation or give you details but, if you see anything strange or think you might be able to help, please contact me.'

'Of course, officer.'

When the door closed behind her, Dixie made a note of the conversation, muttering to herself. How did she guess the motherboard was damaged? How had she come across a similar event? Dixie hadn't. But if she were the saboteur, she would hardly draw attention to herself in that way, would she? Too many questions for now. All we could do was carry on with the investigation.

We found Brett in in his cabin watching a vintage Star Trek film. Dixie explained about the temporary problem with the radiation shield and handed over the tablets. He didn't question Dixie as much as Alina had.

'If you need any help, let me know,' he offered. 'I'm just keen to get back home and see my brother. He's not well, and the medical bills keep coming. He's in a wheelchair now, used to work for Astromin, like us. Saved a man's life once, during a spacewalk. He's a real hero.'

As they talked, I sniffed around. I thought I could smell circuit board, but I didn't find anything out of the ordinary. We stayed to chat for a couple of minutes. I liked Brett. He was always cheerful, helpful and complimentary. He always had a good word to say, about the accommodation, T'unc's food, the crew, pretty much most things.

Next we went to find Jo. She was in her cabin. As Dixie explained the situation I sniffed around, but nothing seemed suspicious. Jo was quite chatty, so we were there a while.

'We had better search the crew cabins, Izzie. Let's start with Jules as he is coming off shift soon.'

Jules' cabin was last on the left. Dixie buzzed in case he was in. No reply, she entered using a special security code.

'OK, Izzie, you know what to do.'

Off I went, there was a faint smell of metal but nothing unusual for an engineer's cabin. There was a strong smell of glue, but I knew Jules liked to build models of old sailing ships. In fact, there was a half built one on his desk. I started sniffing the edges under the bed, the drawers, the cupboard, the desk. Nothing. I looked at Dixie. She nodded towards the en-suite bathroom.

It wasn't a big room, so I found it straight away, a strong scent by the shower, maybe under the shower. I barked my 'found something' bark. Dixie appeared. I pawed the shower rim.

'What have you found, Izzie, let's have a look?' She bent down to examine the trim under the shower.

'Look, these screws have been removed.' She took her Swiss Astronaut Knife from her belt and selected a screwdriver, removing the trim. Once it was off, the scent was stronger. I barked again. Dixie took out her small LED torch and shone it underneath.

'There it is!' The light caught the motherboard glinting near the back. Dixie reached in and grabbed it.

Chapter 14 – A Suspect?

'It's damaged!' Dixie exclaimed. I could see it had been smashed. 'We'd better find Jules.'

As Dixie turned to go, something caught her eye, behind the washstand. It was a small screwdriver. She picked it up.

'Hmm, what's this doing here? Looks like someone's left it. Could be evidence, eh, Izzie. We'll check it for DNA.'

Dixie put the screwdriver in a plastic evidence bag. We called the Captain, then went to find Mo in the engineering control room. She was talking to Smithy. Dixie looked around. No Jules.

'Have you seen Jules?'

'He left twenty minutes ago to get some food, why?' Mo responded, picking up the edge in Dixie's voice.

'I need to ask him some questions. We found the motherboard, damaged, under the shower in his cabin,' she pulled it from her pocket and gave it to Mo. Mo's eyebrows shot up as fast as her jaw dropped.

'You're kidding? No, no, you're not,' she added when she saw Dixie's face. She took the motherboard and examined it. 'I can't leave here right now but I'll call T'unc to alert him.'

'OK. Smithy, you'd better come with me,' said Dixie, loosening the strap on her taser and punching the door button. As we entered the canteen we looked around. No Jules. Dixie walked up to the serving counter. T'unc was waiting for her.

'Hi, Dixie, he left five minutes ago, I think he may have gone to his cabin.'

'Right, T'unc. Come on, Smithy,' she gestured, setting off towards the crew cabins. When they arrived at Jules' cabin, they buzzed. No response. Dixie buzzed again.

'It's locked,' she muttered. Then, raising her voice, 'Jules, it's Dixie, can I have a word please?'

I sat waiting with Dixie. So, it looks like I was barking up the wrong tree when I suspected Dr Zolotov. I thought Jules was suspicious when I smelt him and heard his heart rate. Now we had found the spare motherboard, it seemed an open and shut case. He had access to the ladar unit and could easily have damaged it. Still getting no response, Dixie opened the door with her master security code. As the door slid open it was clear why Jules had not answered. He was face down on the floor. There was some blood on the side of his head. Dixie stepped in and kneeling, felt his pulse.

'He's OK, just out cold. It looks like he was hit from behind.'

I sniffed around for clues as Jules started to stir.

'Easy, Jules.' Dixie put her hand on his shoulder. 'You've had a bad crack on the head.'

Jules groaned and put his hand on the back of his head. He tried to sit up.

'Give it a minute, you will be dizzy for a while. I'll take you to the clinic and check you out.'

Jules nodded, then winced. I sniffed around and went into the bathroom. It looked like someone had been here after we left. I alerted Dixie, who looked and nodded. Dixie and Smithy helped Jules to his feet, steadying him as he walked to the clinic, where Dixie checked him thoroughly and treated his wound.

'What happened, Jules?' Dixie asked.

'Someone hit me from behind. I had had a bite to eat in the canteen, then went back to my cabin. I had literally just walked in when I thought I heard a sound in my bathroom. The next thing I know I'm waking up on the floor with a splitting headache. Someone must have been behind the shower curtain. That's all I know.' He paused. 'What's this about, anyway?'

Dixie explained what we had found hidden under his shower.

'You're joking! Well it wasn't me, why would I do that?' exclaimed Jules. 'But why would they come back? Maybe....'

'Maybe they went back to retrieve this?' Dixie held up the screwdriver. 'We found this in your bathroom. Look, Jules, stay here a while. I need to update the Captain. I'll be back soon.'

As Dixie was briefing the Captain, her wristband beeped. She looked down.

'The search results from Astromin HQ are back. I'll have a look at them at my desk. Then I'll run a DNA check on the screwdriver.'

Dixie sat down and opened the message that had just arrived from Earth. It started with a video from a security controller at Astromin HQ.

'Hi, Dixie, interesting results from your request. For your eyes and ears only, put your headphones on.' The file stopped.

Dixie did so and restarted the file. I couldn't hear but I watched Dixie as the recorded message explained what had been found. Some pictures of passengers came up. These were for the passengers from Earth. She clicked on Dr Zolotov's and it opened. She did a double take. Suddenly Dixie slapped the desk. She took off her headphones.

'Captain,' she called, 'Come and look at this!'

The Captain came over and leant over Dixie's shoulder. 'What have you got, Dixie?'

'Look at him.'

The Captain looked at Dixie's screen to see a middle-aged man, blond hair, blue eyes.

'I don't recognise him.'

'Exactly,' replied Dixie excitedly, 'This is the real Dr Zolotov. So the passenger claiming to be him was clearly a fake. And it's not easy fooling security and hitching a ride on a spaceship like he did. He must have had help. And I bet it was him who sabotaged the ladar.'

'I'll alert Mars. He may still be there. If not, they will need to track him down.'

'Captain!' It was Eva, I could sense the urgency in her voice. 'You'd better come here. We have company!'

Chapter 15 – The Missing Parrot

'Captain, we have another ship on our starboard side.'

The Captain turned to look at the wall screen. 'What's it doing there?' he paused.

'The ship is calling us,' announced Eva.

The ship was on camera now, close enough to see its detail. It looked like a small space barge, except it had no cargo containers.

'Accept, put them on the screen.'

A man's face appeared, middle aged, olive skinned, with a neatly trimmed beard. He was smiling but, strangely, his eyes weren't.

'Hello, Captain, this is Chief Engineer Sasani of the research vessel Europa Explorer. Our instruments detect no ion trail from your ship. We changed course to help. Is everything all right?'

'This is Jim Nokes of the space barge Yuri Gagarin. Thanks for hailing us. We're surprised to see you out here.'

'We're coming back from a research mission on Europa. We've been drilling through the Europan crust, conducting experiments.'

Every specialist space dog (and I expect many of you dear readers) will know that Europa is the third largest moon of Jupiter, slightly smaller than Earth's Moon. It is famous for having the smoothest surface of any natural solid object in the Solar System. Even more amazing is what lies beneath its frozen crust. An underground ocean, which could harbour life. Not life as we know it, but Europan microbes and mini-bugs, maybe, swimming around in their dark, salty, watery home.

The Captain nodded, appearing to accept their explanation. 'Yes, we have a problem with the ion drive. The motherboard is damaged. We have ordered a replacement from Mars.'

'So, I understand, Captain. That's why Astromin asked us to come and see if we could help. Did they not tell you?' The Captain shook his head. Sasani continued, 'Perhaps you should check your mail. What sort of drive is it?'

'A Toshota 2.1.'

'They're usually reliable. Hold on, Captain, I might be able to help.'

The screen went mute as Sasani turned to talk to someone on his left. A short conversation was held. He spoke again.

'Captain, you are in luck. We have a spare 1.9 version motherboard. It should work on your drive, maybe with some reduced functionality, but good enough until you get a replacement. Interested?'

As he said this, he smiled even wider and raised a questioning eyebrow.

'That's a kind offer, Chief, just the news we needed to hear,' replied our Captain, 'Let me consult with my engineer.'

He muted the call and pressed the internal intercom, called Mo and explained the situation.

'Should be no problem,' explained Mo. 'We will lose 10-20% of our performance when accelerating and decelerating but I can make it work. I'll just need to code a couple of computer patches. At least our radiation shields will be working again. It's strange, though, how they've just turned up.'

'I've just checked my mail and, sure enough, Astromin did send me a note to say they contacted them.'

The Captain arranged for the two ships to dock. The research ship had to do the manoeuvring, as we couldn't change course without a working ion drive. We were impressed how well her crew handled their ship and, before long, the Captain, Dixie and I were assembled at the airlock waiting to greet Sasani.

Never, in a million lightyears, could we have guessed what would happen next. The door opened and time seemed to stand still. Standing in front of us was the escaped criminal Sun Tzu, the man who masterminded Dixie's parents' fatal crash. Behind him were five more people, including the so-called Dr Zolotov. Dixie was the first to react, hitting the close button, but she was too late. Zolotov, brandishing a taser, pushed her aside and Sun Tzu strode forward.

'Ah, Captain Nokes,' he gave a sickening smile, 'I am pleased to report that we are taking over your ship.' He gestured to the others, 'Resistance, as they say, is futile.'

He turned to Dixie. 'Well, look who's here. Dixie the troublemaker. Watch her closely, she's the one who caused us all those problems on Mars. Any nonsense from her, eject her from the airlock and she can join her parents. Captain, lead us to the flight deck.'

Dixie's face darkened and her hands clenched. I hoped she wasn't about to try out her new judo moves. The Captain made to speak but one of Sun's thugs pushed him.

'Move!'

As they started down the corridor, Dixie signalled 'stealth mode'. I hung back. Apart from Sasani, Sun and 'Dr Zolotov' there was a woman wearing an engineer's uniform and two heavily built men. I didn't recognise the bald one, but the other's round pock-marked face was unforgettable. It was Zhao, who had sabotaged Dixie's parents' ship.

'What is it you want, Sun?' the Captain demanded.

'Want?' Sun laughed, 'I have it already. Your ship and your cargo.' He turned to Sasani as we passed the engineering control room. He nodded towards the door.

'Sasani, take Vanessa and repair the ion drive. Yuri,' and here he spoke to 'Dr Zolotov', 'Bring the engineer to the flight deck.'

He reached over and pulled Dixie's pass off her tunic, tossing it to Vanessa. 'Here, use this.'

Now it was clear what was going on. We had been boarded by Sun Tzu and his galactic gang of pirates wanting our cargo of rare metals. As we entered the flight deck Eva looked round and took in the situation straight away. Alarm appeared in her face and she made to stand up.

'What the…?'

'Sit,' ordered Sun. He nodded to the intercom. 'Call the rest of the crew and passengers to the flight deck. Tell them nothing, just that they need to attend an emergency meeting.'

Eva hesitated and looked at the Captain.

'Now!' Sun shouted, 'I'm in charge here, not him, do it now!'

Eva obeyed and, before long, all the crew and the three passengers were assembled, standing nervously watching Sun, 'Zolotov' and the two henchmen with their guns aimed at us. I was half hidden behind Dixie's desk and a forest of legs.

'Yuri, are they all here?' Sun asked, 'I don't want to lose any like the last time.'

So he may not be Zolotov, but his name really is Yuri I noted. Yuri counted heads and nodded. Sun turned to the two henchmen. 'Take them to the crew lounge, lock them in,' he commanded.

The Captain stepped forward. 'I protest, it's piracy, you have no right to lock up my crew, you'll…'

Sun thrust his face up to the Captain's, staring eyeball to eyeball. 'What? Do I need a pesky parrot perched on my shoulder or something? Maybe I should say 'ooh-aah, and a bottle of rum, me hearties!' his henchmen chuckled at this. 'Protest all you like, Captain,' he snarled, 'It'll do you no good. And yes, it is piracy.' He nodded to Zhao, 'Take them away and make sure you confiscate their door passes.'

Dixie and the others were marched off to the crew lounge. Sun called after them.

'Any trouble, shoot them!'

I shrank back under the desk, thinking about what I should do next. It was obvious. I ate an abandoned biscuit lying on the floor. Quietly. Stealth mode. I looked around. Ruff, my pet squirrel, was also hiding under the desk. He looked at me accusingly, as if playtime was overdue. I knew I couldn't play now. He would run around the flight deck, squeaking, a dead giveaway.

I lay silently under Dixie's desk, listening to the pirates. I heard Sasani come into the flight deck and talk to Sun, then heard Sun call over the intercom.

'Vanessa, how long before that drive is fixed?'

'About an hour, sir,' came back the reply, 'I'm having trouble recoding and rerouting the older unit.'

'Just hurry up. We need to move this ship out of the shipping lanes before someone realises what's going on. Yuri, Sasani, you stay here, help Vanessa and keep an eye on things, I'm going back to our ship to prepare for the cargo transfer.'

I heard Sun Tzu leave the flight deck by the main door. As I lay there, I began to formulate a plan. Although I was a highly trained, specialist space dog, they had forgotten to train me about how to deal with space pirates. I thought Dixie and the Captain would know what to do but they were locked up. Hang on! A thought stuck me. I still have my pass to open doors. I could go down to the lounge and let them out. Great idea!

But then what? We would have to capture the pirates. How? Aha, obvious, the answer was above my head. The tasers. We would have to take a taser then arrest the pirates. It was the best plan I could think of.

I listened. The two pirates were talking. Leaving Ruff to guard the biscuits, I crept out from under the desk and headed for the door hidden behind the partition. It opened with a slight swish. I stuck my head through and looked down the corridor, listening intently. All clear.

I trotted down to the crew lounge. The door, although locked from the outside, opened as I approached. The Captain had been fiddling with the door control. I think he thought he had opened it.

'Got it,' he called quietly.

I jumped through as the door shut behind me. All eyes turned towards the Captain, then down to me. Dixie spoke first.

'Izzie, you clever dog. You still have your pass.'

'Fine good that will do us,' retorted Jules.

The Captain spoke up. 'At least we have access to the ship now.'

I looked at Dixie, wagging my tail, waiting for her to think about the tasers.

'What we need now are weapons,' added Dixie.

I woofed. Dixie looked at me, puzzled. 'I think Izzie is trying to tell me something.'

I woofed again then jumped up and patted her pocket with my front paws.

'Of course,' beamed Dixie, pulling out the key for the taser cupboard. 'When the taser key went missing, Mo printed another. We have access to the tasers.'

The Captain stood up. 'We can start by taking the flight deck. Come on.'

Dixie put her hand on the Captain's shoulder. 'Hang on, Captain. If we all go, they may hear us before we can grab the tasers. I'll go with Izzie. If I'm successful I'll send her back to fetch you. Then come straight to the flight deck.'

'But please come quietly,' she added

The crew nodded. The door opened. I looked up and down the corridor, all quiet. Dixie stuck her head out.

'Come on, Izzie,' she whispered, setting off.

Chapter 16 – Tables Are Turned

Dixie and I stood and listened. The faint melody of the ship, hardly audible to human ears, seemed to fill the corridor. Along with the whispering, high frequency buzz of electronics, there was now the low frequency drone of the ion drive, which had started again. Everywhere else was quiet. I looked at Dixie. She gestured forwards and we advanced slowly down the corridor. Keeping close to the wall, Dixie's hands left little fingertip smudges on the shiny surfaces. I moved ahead, quietly padding along whilst Dixie tiptoed.

Soon the murmur of conversation from the flight deck was audible. I continued a few more steps, then paused to peer around the corner. Empty. I wagged the 'all clear' stealth code. Dixie knelt to whisper in my ear.

'Izzie, they will see me if I go in.'

She explained what I had to do. Cloak and dagger stuff. I wagged my tail to show I understood. Just what I had trained for. She gave me the key for the gun locker. I crept forward cautiously, key held firmly in my mouth, expecting a door to open any minute and a pirate to spot us. I paused, my ears in hunt mode, and sniffed. Just then the ion drive hum stopped. Maybe they were having problems restarting it.

I knew I had to enter the rear side door of the flight deck, next to Dixie's desk. I could hear an argument break out, so I stepped forward. The door swished open. Surely the pirates heard it! I held my breath. Their conversation continued and was louder now the door was open. They were arguing about the ion drive failure. Dixie stood by the door to make sure it didn't close. I poked my head into her office. Clear. I crept through and looked up. The gun locker was on the wall above Dixie's desk. I had rehearsed it in my head. All I had to do was spring onto her chair, then the desk, stand up with my front paws on the wall and, with the key between my teeth, insert it, turn it, open the lock then drop the key without making a noise, grab a gun, shut the cupboard and escape without being heard. Easy if you're a circus dog, but I wasn't, although I was a pretty resourceful, highly trained, specialist space dog. I figured it couldn't be any harder than an astronaut carrying out maintenance on a spacewalk. But then they had special tools and lots of practice and gun lockers weren't designed to be opened by dogs.

As quietly as a whisper in Space, I sprang onto the chair then the desk. I tried inserting the key. It wouldn't fit! I realised it must be upside down, so I twisted my head the other way and turned. Miraculously, the locker door opened. I gently removed the key and dropped it behind an unopened packet of biscuits. Then I reached up to take a taser, put it carefully down on the desk and nudged the locker door shut. I froze. The pirates were still talking. Gripping the gun in my mouth, I jumped back onto the chair then down to the floor. The gun was heavy and hard to carry and, as I landed, it hit the floor and made a noise.

The pirates stopped talking. There was a pause that seemed to last a long time but was probably only a second or two. I heard Yuri speak.

'Did you hear something?'

'It came from in there.'

I moved under the desk and scrunched up at the back with Ruff. Two pairs of feet came around the corner from the flight deck and stopped. I knew they were looking about the room.

'Look!' said Yuri. I froze, wishing I knew how to fire a taser. Maybe Dixie could save me?

'I see it,' replied Sasani.

I wondered what they had seen, then I saw it too. The packet of biscuits was lying on the floor. It must have fallen off as I jumped. A hand reached down and picked it up.

'Real custard creams from Earth,' Yuri exclaimed, 'Well, they won't be needing these. Hungry?'

'Never say no to a biscuit. Come on. We need to get this drive back online before Sun comes back or we'll be for it!'

They turned to walk back to the flight deck then one of them paused, listening. I could hear Dixie's shallow breathing and her heart pumping hard through the open door.

'It's nothing, come on.'

I waited until they were back at the console talking, then eased myself from under the desk and slipped through the door. Dixie was crouched down, waiting. She took the gun and tickled my ears. I wagged my tail. Then she indicated back down the corridor and I raced back to the crew lounge.

As the door opened, the Captain was waiting. Telling the passengers to stay put, he led the crew back to the flight deck. By the time we arrived, Dixie had Yuri and Sasani under guard, threatened by the taser.

'Well done, Dixie,' congratulated the Captain. 'Jules, Smithy, handcuff them. The cuffs are in Dixie's drawer.'

'What about the others?' Jules asked, as he cuffed Sasani.

'Vanessa and the bald one were in engineering trying to fix the ion drive. I think Sun and Zhao went back to their ship.'

'OK, Mo. You and Eva undock the ship. Dixie, Jules, T'unc, we'll go to engineering.'

Before long, Vanessa and her fellow pirate were sitting, handcuffed, in the corner of the flight deck along with Yuri and Sasani. The Captain took charge.

'Mo, send a distress signal and a message to Astromin HQ about the situation.' Mo nodded and turned back to the console. 'Eva, have we undocked from the pirate ship?'

'Yes, Captain.'

'Captain,' it was Mo, 'Our signals are being jammed.'

Just then the video screen flashed into life. Sun Tzu's scowling face appeared. 'You are being very foolish, Captain. You will regret this.'

'You should surrender your ship now, Sun,' replied the Captain.

Sun laughed, lent forward and switched off. Dixie spoke first.

'I don't know why he's so cocky. We have his crew and our ship. There is nothing he can do.'

The Captain nodded. 'Jules, tell the passengers it's safe now. T'unc, we could all do with some food. Mo, get the ion drive back online. Smithy, Dixie, put these criminals into a spare cabin, keep them cuffed.'

In no time, the ion drive was fully operational, although communications were still jammed. We could see the pirate ship about 2000 metres off the port side. We only had one option now, to continue towards Mars. At least we had our magnetic shield working again so space radiation sickness wasn't a concern.

T'unc took the prisoners some food and Dixie checked they were secure for the night. We retired to our cabins for a well-earned night's sleep.

Dogs don't sleep heavily so, when the ship shuddered at about two in the morning, I was immediately alert. I went over to Dixie and jumped on her bunk, pawing her and barking my emergency bark. She sat up like a jack in a box, fully alert.

'What is it, Izzie?'

The ship was quiet now. I growled my warning growl. Dixie listened, puzzled, then sprang out of bed. She looked out of her window.

'Izzie, we're in trouble. The pirate ship has docked with us. Something's wrong. I'll call the Captain.'

The Captain came on the intercom sounding sleepy. Dixie explained.

'How can that be?' the Captain sounded astounded. 'We'd better get to the flight deck and lock down the ship, I'll meet you there.'

Dixie dressed in record time and punched the button to open the door into the corridor. As it opened the pock-marked face of Zhao greeted us. He pushed Dixie back into the cabin.

'Ah, Officer Symon, I was just coming to give you your wake-up call.'

Zhao spun Dixie round and handcuffed her before she had time to react. Dixie shot me a warning glance.

'Get lost!'

'Huh,' he laughed, 'Too late for that.'

I knew Dixie was talking to me. I made myself scarce.

Zhao pushed Dixie into the corridor and towards the flight deck. Leaving Ruff on my bed, I followed at a distance, entered through the side door and hid under Dixie's desk. I could hear Eva was there too.

Sun Tzu arrived. 'Round up all the crew and passengers and take them to the crew lounge, this time make sure they are all handcuffed. Good work, Brett. I knew it was sensible to have an inside man as a backup. You did a good job releasing my crew and re-docking. We owe you a debt of gratitude.'

So Brett was a pirate too. And I liked him, well, not any more obviously. We had taken him on board posing as a mining engineer on his way home. Maybe he was. In any case, he was a traitor.

'No problem, Sun, you pay a lot better than the mining company, and I need the money for my brother's medical bills.'

I shrank further under the desk, listening, waiting.

Chapter 17 −Voice in the Kitchen

In the time it takes for a squirrel to shin up a tree, the crew had been assembled in the crew lounge, handcuffed. Vanessa and Zhao brought Jo and Alina. Alina was protesting.

'Hold your tongue!' Vanessa spat.

'How dare you treat me like this, I'm a passenger on this ship,' Alina complained, struggling.

'I said shut up!' growled Vanessa, punching Alina in the stomach. Alina grunted and doubled up as Vanessa pushed her into the room. Sun Tzu strode in and looked around.

'All here?'

'Yes, sir,' answered Zhao, 'All cuffed as you ordered.'

'OK, you stand guard outside the door. The others have started unloading the cargo. Vanessa, you come with me.'

With that they left, Zhao shut the door and took up his position in the corridor.

I had escaped the notice of the pirates, which was a good start, but with Zhao guarding the lounge it would be impossible to free the crew again. Nearly as bad, there was no-one to feed me! I knew there was only one thing to do. Head for the kitchen to see if I could find some food.

I listened for movement It was quiet, so I stuck my head into the passenger corridor. Empty. I made a dash for the kitchen. The door opened as I approached but I hung back in case anyone was in there. I waited. No sounds, just the normal hum, so I entered. After taking a long drink from my bowl, I looked around for food. I knew I couldn't open the fridge (anyway, the fridge and I don't get on, as you know) but I could open one of the lower cupboards. I went to the one where the custard creams were kept and, in the time it took to woof 'hooray!', I had opened a packet and was eating one or two. OK, a few, well several really. I stopped and looked around me. It was a mess, bits of packet, a broken biscuit (oh, nope, that's gone now), crumbs and so on. It would be a give-away if the pirates found it. I started to lick up the crumbs.

'Psst, Izzie.'

I stopped licking the floor, ears up, moving from side to side to locate the sound.

'Izzie, up here!'

I looked up to the ceiling. A face was grinning down from an open air vent.

'Dan?' I woofed, tail wagging.

Dan put his finger to his lips. 'Shhh! Quiet!'

Dan levered himself through the vent hole, lowering his body down to the work surface. His biceps bulged and he looked in good shape. He jumped nimbly down to the floor. My tail was swishing from side to side and I was skipping with excitement.

'Izzie, calm down, you look like you'll take off wagging your tail like that!'

Dan patted my head, and I licked his nose. I was really pleased to see him. He chuckled then turned serious.

'I know what's been going on. We need to rescue Dixie and the crew. I heard that Brett was one of them. Don't worry,' here Dan smiled his 'it's all under control' grin, 'I have a plan. First we need to clear up this mess.' He pointed to the remains of the biscuits. 'Actually, I think I'll have a couple, I'm starving.'

Dan explained the plan. First we had to deal with Zhao. I went towards the canteen door that opened into the crew corridor. I stayed where I was as it opened. I couldn't see Zhao, but I could hear his breathing and see his shadow from the bulkhead light. I waited. For a few seconds nothing happened then Zhao called out.

'Who's there?'

I stood still.

'Anyone there?' He started walking toward the open door, then he saw me.

'You! What are you doing here? I thought we had locked you up.' He laughed, 'Want to go back in the fridge?'

I sat a few feet inside the door, wagging my tail. As Zhao bent down to grab my collar, he didn't see the heavy fire extinguisher that Dan brought down hard on his head. The pirate fell heavily, spread-eagled across the floor, out cold.

'Good work, Space Dog. Let's drag him over to the crew lounge.'

Dan grabbed Zhao by the ankle and dragged him down the corridor. I trotted the short way to the crew lounge door. It opened. All eyes turned to look, then they moved down to look at me.

'Izzie?' queried Dixie, getting up out of her seat, 'Where's Zhao? How have you.....?'

Her voice tailed off as Dan's smiling face appeared at the side of the door.

'Quit yapping, Dixie, and give me a hand here,' he grinned.

He started pulling Zhao into the room. Dixie just stood there dumbstruck, her mouth opening and closing. Then she recovered herself and grabbed Zhao's other ankle. The door slid shut.

'Dan, how did you…?'

Dan grabbed Dixie around her waist and gave her a big kiss on the cheek and a hug.

'Good to see you too, sis. Hi, everyone,' he added, addressing the rest of the room. Dixie pushed Dan back, holding his arm.

'Dan, it's great to see you. Hey, everyone, this is Dan.' Most people nodded; they had figured that out.

Dixie shook her head in disbelief, 'But how did you get on board?' she asked as she knelt and felt through Zhao's pockets to find the handcuff key, unlocked her cuffs then the Captain's, who took the key and started releasing the others.

'I knew I had been framed for that theft and had to leave the asteroid, so I stole a survival suit and anchored myself to a container. Honestly, it was terrifying while you were accelerating but after a few hours I was able to let myself in through the cargo deck air lock.'

'So it wasn't a fault after all,' interrupted Mo. 'You must have nerves of steel! It's good to see you again, Dan,' she added, blushing slightly.

'Hi, Mo. Once I was in, I hid the suit and stayed on the cargo deck, apart from a quick trip to the kitchen and the clinic. Sorry, Dixie, I needed the anti-radiation tablets after being outside for so long. I didn't realise you would all need them too.'

'Of course, that makes sense now,' smiled Dixie, 'You're right Dan, you'll need a high dose for at least a week to minimise any radiation sickness.'

'Anyway, we don't have time for chitchat. I heard what was going on. The pirates plan to steal your precious metal cargo then blow up the ship, with you in it, just like they did with my ship, though in that case it was gas they were after to refuel their ship,' Dan added grimly.

The Captain spoke up. 'You mean your ship's explosion wasn't an accident?'

'No way! It was cold blooded piracy and murder. They boarded the ship, locked up the crew and stole a tank of gas. I was checking the escape shuttles when they boarded, so they missed me. I heard them set the explosives but there was nothing I could do, they had put the ship into auto lockdown. I escaped seconds before the explosion. I don't think the pirates realised. I must have been out of sight of their ship and hidden by the explosion debris.'

The Captain interrupted. 'Well, it's good to have you on board, Dan. What's the situation out there?'

'This deck is clear. I think there are two or three pirates on their ship, the rest are on the cargo deck moving the metal pods from the containers.'

Smithy spoke up. 'I saw them take our tasers so we only have one weapon,' pointing to the pirate's holster, 'Is that enough?'

'We can print more,' Mo interjected, 'On the 3D printer in engineering, at least a simple one, but it'll work if we can find some cartridges.'

'I should have magazines in my office,' offered Dixie.

Dan punched Mo gently on the shoulder. 'Print a gun. Cool, let's go.'

'Wait!' came a voice from the back of the room.

Chapter 18 – The Detective

It was Alina who spoke, the research scientist who had joined the ship at Thisbe. All eyes turned to look at her. She continued.

'It seems time to declare myself. I'm an undercover officer with the Federal Space Rangers. I have been tracking this gang for a while. I can help now.'

The Captain and Dixie exchanged glances. Dixie spoke first.

'Given the circumstances, how can you prove who you are?'

'You know as well as I do, Dixie, but obviously not in front of everyone.'

Dixie nodded towards a corner of the room. 'Over there.'

Dixie, Alina and I went into the corner and they started whispering. It turned out that each of them had half an encrypted password, recognised by Rangers and security officers. They exchanged the two halves through their wristbands to verify who the other person was.

Dixie turned back to the room. 'That's confirmed, Captain, Alina's one of us.'

The Captain smiled, 'Excellent, we can use all the help we can get.'

Now Jo, the other passenger who was sitting in the corner, spoke up. 'That just leaves me. I really am a passenger, but I'll do what I can to help.'

The Captain turned to Jo. 'Thanks Jo, but we can't put a passenger in any danger. Let us deal with this situation and maybe you can help later, all right?'

Jo nodded, 'Whatever you say, Captain, just ask.'

The Captain looked around the room. 'All clear on what we are doing?'

Everyone nodded. I woofed.

'Right,' said Dixie, 'Mo, Izzie, let's go!'

We picked up the taser cartridges and headed to engineering. Mo was downstairs at the printer. She had selected the taser recipe, added the print cartridges and switched it on. It took about five minutes to print the gun. As soon as the new taser was cool enough to hold, Dixie slipped in a magazine, raised the gun and fired at a chair. Blue light flashed and crackled across the surface as it discharged.

'Works a treat,' nodded Dixie approvingly, 'Good work, Mo.'

Mo beamed. 'Let's get back to the lounge then.'

When we returned to the lounge Zhao was still out cold but now he was trussed up and gagged. Dixie held up the taser, the Captain smiled. He held up the one he had taken from Zhao.

'Good work. OK, Dixie, Dan, Jules, T'unc, Alina, you come with me. Eva, Mo, Smithy, get this ship and the comms back online as soon as I call you from the cargo deck. Let's go.'

We stopped to check the cargo deck cameras. We could see Sasani and the bald baddy, using the controls to manoeuvre our small space tug, the size of a large refrigerator, between the two ships. It looked like Brett was in a space suit inside a container, helping to move the precious metals.

'We'll have to take the steps down, they'll hear the lift. Dixie and I will go first, then Dan, then the rest of you. Keep it quiet.'

We went down into the engineering workshop. The Captain stopped at the door to the cargo deck and peered through the window.

'They're both at the docking computer, on the left. Dixie, no messing, taser them, no questions asked. You take the one on the left, I'll go first.'

The Captain slowly opened the door. Sasani must have sensed something because, as the Captain burst out from the door opening, he lifted his taser and fired before the Captain could. The Captain fell twitching to the floor. His taser fell beside him. Dixie was quicker and fired at Sasani, bringing him down. Baldy snatched up his gun from the desk. He raised it to aim.

I think now might be a good time to explain why Alfie the Alsatian beat me by a whisker to first place at the Space Academy. He scored more points than me in the 'grab a person with a gun' exercise. That part of my training was not my strong point as I'm quite a lot smaller than an Alsatian. However, my Academy instructor would have been proud of me had she been watching now. Baldy raised his gun and, as he did so, I leapt, locking my jaws around his wrist. He yelled in pain and tried to shake me off. Ten kilograms of angry space dog with a vice-like grip hanging onto your wrist can be a distraction.

We fell to the ground, a writhing bundle of bawling baddy and persistent pooch. Dixie and Alina jumped on Baldy and before long he was restrained. Dan stood by with the Captain's taser levelled.

'Good work, Izzie, Alina,' Dixie said, rubbing my head. 'Let's get these two tied up, I'll see to the Captain.'

Dixie went over to the Captain and flicked the taser cartridge away with her gun, then felt his pulse. It was racing but not dangerously high. Dixie cradled his head in her arms. The Captain's eyelids started to flicker. He would take a while to come round. Dan came over and touched her shoulder.

'Those two are trussed up,' he announced adding, with concern in his voice, 'Will the Captain be OK?'

'Sure, T'unc and Jules can take him to the clinic and keep him under observation. We still have four more pirates to capture.'

As T'unc and Jules helped the Captain, Dixie turned to the docking computer. Brett was asking what was going on.

Dixie spoke into the microphone. 'Brett, we have your two friends under arrest, you'd better come in, just don't try anything.'

There was a long silence, then Brett spoke. 'You've got to be joking. I'm heading back to our ship, then you'll be sorry you took us on.'

Dixie could see Brett push himself off the container and start to drift towards the pirate's ship.

'I'm not having that,' Dixie muttered.

She grabbed the controls for the tug and turned it towards Brett. As the tug accelerated, leaving little puffs of gas behind, Brett turned and realised the danger he was in. The tug hit him squarely but, before he could react, it had grabbed his arm. Both the tug and Brett moved away into the emptiness of space. As they left the ship's shadow they were lit up by sunlight. They became smaller and smaller, tumbling slowly in space, glinting as they caught the sunlight, until they were a mere speck on the screen. Alina looked quizzically at Dixie.

'Don't worry, Alina, he's heading for Mars. We can pick him up in an hour or so when we have things sorted here. He'll have learnt not to mess with us.'

Dan high fived Dixie, 'Nice one, sis.'

Alina interrupted. 'Can you two stop admiring each other. We need to board the pirate ship before they realise something is up.'

'You're right,' Dixie replied. 'These two will be safe here. Alina, grab Sasani's gun. Come on.'

We moved warily to the airlock connecting the two ships. Dixie stopped, listened, then stepped into the pirate's ship. She gave the thumbs up and skipped across the corridor, flattening herself against the bulkhead. She signalled to me.

'You know what to do, Izzie. Wait until I'm ready.'

I wagged my tail to show I understood.

Chapter 19 – Sun Down

I walked into the corridor and barked. I kept barking until I saw someone coming. It was Yuri.

'What's going on?' yelled Sun Tzu from behind a door.

'It's that dog. Thought it was done for when I shut it in the fridge! I don't know where it came from but I'm gonna enjoy tasering it.' Yuri took his gun out of his holster and starting walking towards me. I backed away and went back into the hatch. He followed and, as he raised his taser, he crumpled and fell as Dixie fired from behind. Dan and Alina grabbed him and pulled him into our ship, handcuffing him and forcing a gag between his clenched teeth.

'Good work, you two. Now let's find the other two,' Dan grinned.

We advanced purposefully back up the corridor. We could hear Sun Tzu talking to Vanessa.

'Vanessa, I can't raise the cargo deck, something must be wrong. Go with Yuri and check it out. Be careful.'

'Right, boss, on my way.'

I could hear Vanessa moving towards the door. Alina pushed past Dixie and Dan.

'This one's mine,' she growled, 'You take Sun.'

Just then Vanessa came through the door, turned into the corridor and saw us. Her taser was already raised and, before anyone could react, she fired at Alina. To everyone's surprise, and Vanessa's obvious shock judging by her expression, Alina just kept moving. Before Vanessa could fire again, Alina had landed a hefty kick in Vanessa's midriff that sent her flying backwards into the bulkhead with a large thud. She collapsed in a heap on the floor.

Dixie, Dan and I entered the pirate's flight deck. It was small. Sun must have heard the commotion outside and was ready for us. He ducked behind a console as I flew up at him, snarling. He fired but I put him off his aim. Dan saw it coming and leapt to one side, dodging the cartridge, just as Dixie fired. Her shot caught Sun Tzu on the cheek and he grimaced in pain, collapsing into a whimpering heap. I stood over him, growling. Dixie and Dan walked behind the console.

'Well done, Izzie. Now stand back,' said Dixie, handing me a treat.

We waited for the cartridge to finish discharging before Dan rolled Sun Tzu over and handcuffed him. Alina looked over the top of the console, smiling.

'Great work, team. Vanessa's tied up, so we have them all.'

Dan turned, jubilant, and smiled. 'Hey, Alina, you were lucky that taser didn't affect you. Must have been a dud.'

'No luck in it, Dan, look,' she lifted her T-shirt to reveal a skin-tight suit underneath.

'Lycra? You're kidding,' replied Dan.

'Not Lycra. It's one of the new issue anti-taser suits made from Kevlar and carbon nanotubes. The electricity discharged by the taser is channelled harmlessly down to the floor through the suit and my boots.'

'Cool, I've got to have one of those,' Dixie responded.

We soon had the pirates assembled on the cargo deck and Dixie and I went to check the Captain. T'unc and Jules were there making the Captain comfortable on one of the beds.

'I tell you, I'm fine,' the Captain was saying.

'Can I be the judge of that?' Dixie interrupted.

'Honestly, Dixie, I feel like I have cramp in my left leg and I'm a little lightheaded, but I'm fine.' He tried to get up, wobbled and sat down again.

'Well, maybe a bit dizzy. What's the situation, Dixie?'

'All the pirates are captured, except for Brett who is heading towards Mars with the tug.'

'Well, I suppose we had better bring him back, not sure he deserves it though. Tempted not to.'

Dixie turned to T'unc and Jules. 'Thanks, you two. T'unc, I guess we could all do with some food, maybe. Jules, update Mo, will you?'

As they left, Dixie hooked the Captain up to a monitor. It beeped and flashed and, before long, the screen showed the results.

'All seems OK, Captain.' Dixie reached into a cupboard. 'Have this energy drink then see how you feel.'

The Captain drank up and soon stood without any trouble. He limped back to the flight deck. Eva, Mo, Jules, Alina and Dan were there.

'Captain, Alina's just sent a message to the Federal Space Rangers at Mars Orbiter so they know our situation. They'll be there to remove our, er, unwanted cargo. I do have one concern though.' Dan paused uncertainly, looking more serious than usual.

The Captain raised an eyebrow, 'And that is......?'

'I think the pirates may have planted a bomb on our ship.'

All the pirates were held in a spare cabin, handcuffed and bound tightly. Jules stood guard outside. The Captain went in, with Dixie, me and Dan.

'Sun,' the Captain started, 'Alina has been in touch with the Federal Space Rangers and they'll be meeting us at Mars. Dan thinks you may have planted explosives on the ship. Is that true? If you help us now, the Galactic Court may be more lenient.'

Sun sneered but said nothing. The Captain continued. 'Understand this, Sun, I'm not putting my crew at risk. You can cooperate or face the consequences.'

'I have nothing to say to you,' Sun spat.

The Captain nodded and indicated we should leave. Outside the Captain spoke again.

'Dixie, you and Izzie need to start a search of the ship. Dan, round up Jo and the rest of the crew and take them to the pirate ship. Then undock and stand off at 5000 metres.'

'OK, sir, but if it's all the same to you I'll stay on board and help Dixie. I specialised in electronics at the academy after all. Anyway, I can't let Dixie have all the fun.'

The Captain paused, looking Dan in the eye. 'OK, but only once everyone else is safe on board the other ship.'

'Ay, Captain, consider it done.' Dan headed off to round everyone up.

'Start on the cargo deck, Dixie. As soon as you find anything let me know. I'll start in the passenger cabins.'

We headed down to the cargo deck. As a highly trained, specialist space dog I knew what to do. I stuck my nose into every corner. I crawled into tight spaces, all the time sniffing. Dixie would open containers for me to check. After thirty minutes or so I had found nothing. The radio crackled into life.

'Captain, this is Dan, everyone is aboard the other ship and Eva is moving into position as you ordered. Where do you want me to start?'

'I've nearly completed the cabins. I'll do the lounges if you search the canteen and kitchen.'

'Roger that, Captain.'

'Captain, Izzie and I have drawn a blank down here, I'll bring Izzie up there to help.'

'Thanks, Dixie.'

We moved up to the main deck and met Dan in the kitchen.

'Maybe they have hidden the bomb somewhere to disguise its smell, like with coffee,' Dan suggested.

'Well, let's give the place a good going over. Izzie won't be fooled by that.'

We all started searching the cupboards until the radio crackled again.

'Captain, this is Eva. I think I can see the bomb, at least there is something attached to the outside of the ship, just above the flight deck.'

There was a pause. 'OK, Eva, we'll investigate. Dixie, Dan, meet me on the flight deck.'

We arrived just before the Captain. Dixie called up an outside camera. It picked out the detail of the ship, one array of solar cells shining on the sunward side, the other in deep shadow. Stretching forwards were the rails used by astronauts to attach safety ropes during a spacewalk. Either side were small pieces of equipment and the tanks containing the toxic chemicals used for the air conditioning system and the waste recycling processes, as well as the spare oxygen tanks. Dixie zoomed the image.

'Looks like there may be something there, but with the flight deck sloping down to the front of the ship, I can't see well. It's a bit of a blind spot. Brett must have placed it there when he was outside. Maybe we shouldn't bother picking him up on the way back,' Dixie added grimly.

'I'll go out and take a look,' offered Dan.

'No need,' replied Dixie, 'We can use our remote probe.'

She turned to another screen and called up a picture showing a probe the size of a microwave oven. A few clicks and the image changed to what was obviously the view from the probe's camera. Using a joystick, Dixie moved the probe along the deck. It came into view in the first monitor, skimming slowly over the sunlit surface of the ship, its safety and communication umbilical cable trailing lazily behind it. In no time it was close to the object.

It was the Captain who spoke first. 'It looks like a decompression bomb, designed to punch a hole in the hull, too big for the auto-seal to repair but small enough to look like an asteroid impact when the investigators put the ship's pieces together, if they ever can. The ship will decompress and break up with hardly a trace. It looks like it's held on magnetically. This could be tricky. If we de-energise the magnet the bomb will probably go off before we can remove it.'

'There is a way,' explained Dixie, 'We need to attach a power source across the trigger terminals whilst we disable the magnet. I can do that with Dan's help. We need to go outside.'

The Captain hesitated. We all knew that space walks were never allowed if there was any possibility of solving a problem like this using remote probes.

Dan chipped in. 'It's a no-brainer, Captain.'

The Captain nodded grimly. 'Come on then, I'll help you suit up.'

I woofed excitedly. I love a spacewalk.

'Not you, Izzie, you stay with me.'

Chapter 20 – Space Walk

We all went down to the cargo deck where the spacesuits were kept. Dan and Dixie were suited and booted in record time.

'OK, you two, you have enough air for two hours which should be plenty. Make sure your safety ropes stay tied onto the rails. Dixie, you have the power source. Dan, here is the power tool you'll need. Lift your arm and I'll attach the tether.'

Dan obliged and tucked the tool into the holster on his suit, moving into the airlock with Dixie. The door closed behind them. I woofed good luck.

The Captain and I watched as the airlock lights turned red and the outer door opened, flooding the deck with sunlight. Dixie and Dan left the ship, tethered by their safety ropes. The outer airlock door closed behind them.

The Captain spoke. 'Come on, Izzie, up to the flight deck.'

Before long, we were sitting at the console watching the images of the outside. The Captain had lifted me onto the desk so I could see what was happening. He spoke through the radio.

'We're on the flight deck, we have you both on visual.'

'Roger that, we're almost there.'

It was too nerve-wracking to enjoy the crisp images of the stars and nebulae in the background. The bomb could go off any moment. We watched breathlessly as Dixie and Dan inched their way along the top of the ship. Every so often they had to unhook themselves to move around some equipment and, at the same time, avoid the probe's cable, which was wandering gently in space. Soon they were next to the bomb, examining it from all angles. It was Dan who spoke first.

'External power source. I can see the panel we need to take off, unscrewing it now.'

We watched as Dan removed the screws one by one, carefully putting them in a magnetic holder, followed by the cover. They couldn't risk losing parts into space, as even tiny parts were a danger to ships moving at our speed.

'OK, I can see the magnet terminals and the firing mechanisms. Dixie, put your battery across these two terminals here to provide the temporary power to the firing mechanism.'

We could see what was happening through the probe's camera, which was hovering about two metres away. Dixie took her battery and, with steady hands, attached it to the terminals.

'Right,' said Dan, a little nervously I thought, 'Let's shutdown the magnet power source. I'll cut this cable.'

He cut it, I closed my eyes and waited. A sigh of relief came over the intercom. Dan nudged the bomb and it lifted slowly off the ship. He grabbed it. Dixie spoke.

'Good work, Dan. We need to discharge it out here, we can't risk it going off inside. We'll have to fire the projectile into space, away from the shipping lanes. We can tether the rest of the bomb to the ship to stop it flying in the opposite direction.'

'OK, Dixie, that's a good plan, hey, what's happening..... this red light's started to blink.'

The blinking became faster and faster. The Captain shouted.

'Watch out, it's going to…'

Before he could finish his sentence, the bomb went off. There was a bright flash but, in the vacuum of space, no sound. The projectile flashed past Dixie into space. At the same time the rest of the bomb mechanism flew in the other direction. It crashed into the front of Dan's spacesuit, smashing his life support box and shooting him into space. His rope jerked him to an abrupt stop and he rebounded, crashing into the side of the ship. Alarms started going off in the flight deck.

'Dixie, Dan's life support is critically damaged. Get him back now!'

'I know, I'm on it.'

Dixie pushed herself over to Dan, 'His umbilical is leaking, and the spare connector socket is smashed. I can't use my pack to support him.'

She grabbed Dan and attached his lanyard to her suit. We could see his visor was steaming up, indicating loss of suit pressure. She unclipped her lanyard and pulled herself along the safety railings at a dangerous speed, punching the probe out of the way, Dan trailing limply and lifelessly behind, bouncing off the roof.

'I'll open the airlock,' the Captain called, as he ran from the flight deck, Dan's life support alarms still blaring. We were there in record time. Seconds later Dixie climbed in and Dan fell onto the floor behind her. The Captain shut the outer door and pressed the emergency repressurisation button. In moments, the lights had changed to green, the inner door was open, and he was taking Dan's helmet off. Dan's face was blue. He was struggling to breathe. Dixie took off her helmet, her expression one of anguish. She was shaking from the adrenaline rush, due to exertion or emotion or both.

'Dan. DAN. Speak to me.'

'I'm, ouch, I'm........ OK,' Dan gasped, struggling to catch his breath, 'I think…. I think I may have cracked a rib…oooh…. or two. Aaah, I feel sick.'

I woah-woahed in delight and licked his face. Dixie wiped a tear from her eye, smiling and laughing. That was no simulation out there. It had been a close call, a whisker from death.

'Trust you,' she said lovingly.

Dixie insisted Dan was cut out of his suit because of his injuries, which might be more serious than he thought. Cutting up a spacesuit is no easy task, but he was soon out of it and being stretchered up to the clinic.

'Captain, I need to look after Dan. He'll need a scan and painkillers. I think you should ask Eva to re-dock, we could use some help.'

'Good idea, Dixie, I'm on my way.'

Before long, the two ships were docked. Mo was the first person to come and see Dan.

'How is he, Dixie?' she asked with obvious concern in her voice, 'We watched the whole thing from the other ship. I've never seen anyone move as fast as you did to bring Dan back in. You were taking quite a risk there, you know, unclipped.'

'I'm worth it though, Mo,' Dan chuckled. 'Ow, I mustn't laugh. Don't make me laugh.'

'As you can see, Mo, he's fine. Two cracked ribs and some nasty bruising but he seems to have avoided any decompression problems or internal injury. I've conducted a full scan and given him painkillers.'

Mo took Dan's hand. 'I was really worried about you, you know,' she blushed.

'It'll take more than that to make a dent in me, Mo, but look, I know I've been beyond lucky.' Dan winced and paused for breath. 'When I escaped from the Buzz Aldrin I was caught in the explosion. If I had left half a minute later, I probably wouldn't be here. Even so, the explosion seriously damaged the shuttle I was in.' Another pause, 'The alarm panel lit up like a Christmas tree, so I knew I was in trouble. I managed to save power by switching off most circuits and turning the temperature right down, but I reckon I only just made it. I had water and basic rations but if that ship from Vela hadn't found me, well.......I owe them my life.'

'Do you remember what happened on Thisbe, Dan?' Dixie asked.

'I remember waking up in their clinic with a drip attached, then dozing off again before they woke me to accuse me of stealing some electronic card and software. I didn't do it, you know.'

'Of course you didn't, Dan, but we'll need proof,' Dixie pointed out.

Now being a highly trained, specialist space dog, 'proof' is a word that makes me sit up. I thought I might know where we could find proof. I woofed. They all looked at me as I turned, halting at the door and woofing again.

'Izzie's onto something, I think. Mo, you stay here with Dan while I check this out.'

I ran down the passenger corridor and stopped outside Brett's cabin. Dixie caught up. We went inside, nose in hunt mode. I sniffed around the bed and drawers then went over to the cupboard, wagging my tail. Dixie opened it and I sniffed inside. Aha, I thought, grabbing a ruck sack in my teeth and dragging it out.

'Look in here,' I woofed.

Dixie knelt and opened the rucksack, tipping the contents onto the floor. A small plastic case the size of a playing card caught her eye.

'Well done, Izzie, this is a stealth case. Very expensive and invisible to scanners.' She opened the case. 'Look what we have here, the missing card from the mine.'

'More,' I woofed, nudging the pack with my nose.

'Let's see what else we have.'

Dixie rifled through the heap and stopped to pick up a tablet computer. She switched it on and searched for recent files. One, a video, attracted her attention. It showed the Thisbe mine machine room and it appeared to be a copy of the one the mine manager had shown her of Dan stealing the card and software.

'Hmm,' Dixie muttered, 'How come this video is on this tablet?'

She continued to look at the recent files and opened another video. This was an identical video except this time it was clearly Brett in the film, not Dan.

'So that's how he did it, Izzie. Brett doctored the video showing him stealing the card and software by superimposing Dan's face instead of his. Well done, Izzie, we have all the proof we need to clear Dan's name and lock up Brett for a long time. That reminds me, we need to pick him up before he runs out of air. Come on, let's tell the others the good news and send a message to Thisbe and Astromin HQ to tell them we found the card and software.'

That evening, with Brett picked up and locked away with the others, we all tucked into a huge celebratory curry T'unc had cooked. Well, all except me, because curries don't agree with me, so T'unc gave me some cooked chicken and rice and some dog biscuits. The mood was cheerful. Everyone was swapping stories and reliving the events of the last couple of days. I was going to tell Ruff, my robotic pet squirrel, all about it later. After a while Dixie spoke up.

'Should we give the prisoners some food, Captain?' That's my Dixie, always concerned for others, whoever they are.

'Yes, I suppose we ought to. Smithy, Alina, please go with T'unc but don't unlock the prisoners' cuffs, they can eat their food as best they can.'

Chapter 21- Old Friends

The next morning things appeared normal, except we were short of crew. Eva, Jules and Smithy were crewing the pirate ship back to Mars Orbiter, flying a few kilometres ahead of us. As we approached the space station, we could see two empty docks reserved for us. Eva docked the pirates' ship, then we went in. It wasn't long before the doors were open and the Captain, Dixie, me and Alina were waiting for the Rangers to come aboard. We heard their boots coming down the corridor, three of them. The first was our old friend, Jack Turner, who had helped us save the Mars Galileo Base from Sun Tzu's gang. Dixie waved and I wagged but, before we knew it, he was hugging Alina.

'I'm glad you're OK,' he said, kissing her, before turning to give Dixie a hug and me a pat. The Captain raised his eyebrows. Alina explained.

'My husband, Captain.'

Jack saluted then held out his hand to the Captain. The Captain took it.

'I'm Captain Jack Turner, sir. You and your team have done a great job capturing this lot, we've been after them a while, which is why we sent our ace detective on the trail.' Alina smiled, colouring a little.

'We knew there was someone on Thisbe stealing secrets,' added Alina, 'That's why I was there. I wasn't sure it was Brett though, until it was too late.'

Jack waved to the other two rangers nearby, nodding towards where the prisoners were being held. 'OK, go with Alina, arrest them and lock them up securely. Don't take any chances.'

As they left, Jack turned to Dixie. 'I understand you have an injured man on board. I heard it might be Dan?' Dixie nodded. 'The medics will be here shortly, and we can transfer him to our clinic. How is he?'

'He's been through a lot, but he'll bounce back.'

We watched as the Rangers came back with the pirates, still handcuffed. As they shuffled past, Sun turned to Dixie.

'Don't think this is the end of it, Symon.'

'Quiet there,' Alina commanded, 'Or you'll be gagged.'

Sun turned as he was led away. We watched them disappear around the corner, almost bumping into a man in full moon glasses coming to meet us.

'Gautier!' called Dixie, grabbing Gautier's hand, 'Good to see you. What are you doing here?'

Gautier was the commander of Galileo Base when we saved it from Sun Tzu's attack a few months earlier.

'Hello, everyone,' he beamed. 'I came to congratulate you on capturing Sun Tzu. Well done. We'll make sure he is secure here until he is taken to Earth for trial. I also came to welcome you onto my space station. I have been promoted and now run Mars Orbiter.'

'Congratulations,' smiled Dixie.

'And I have more news. The company wants to award everyone a medal, and Izzie too. The pirates' ship has been impounded and will be sold, probably converted into a freighter to replace the Buzz Aldrin, so there'll be a bonus for you all as well.'

'All I care about is that we have captured the people who murdered our parents. I hope they throw away the key! And I think Izzie would just be happy with a big treat,' replied Dixie, looking down at me.

'Treat, mmmmm,' I woofed.

We went with Dan as the medics wheeled him to the station's clinic. Dan complained there was nothing wrong with him (ouch! well just the odd niggle here and there, he added, and - ooh - don't make me laugh, please!). The medic told him he would have to stay in the clinic overnight.

'Well, Dixie, that was some adventure.'

Dixie turned to see the Captain, smiling and rubbing his beard.

'Yes, sir, it was. All's well that ends well.'

The next day we removed our cargo of precious metal from the pirates' ship, reloading it into our containers. We were due to return to Lunar Orbiter Alpha. From there, space shuttles would take the cargo down to the Astromin base east of London. Here the metals would be refined further and shipped to Europe and America. We would pick up new supplies for Mars and the mines, then start a new voyage. As Dixie, Ruff and I stood watching the last of the cargo transfer, she turned to me.

'Izzie, you are looking really shaggy! I think you need a haircut.'

I wagged my tail. I like to be groomed. I like the attention. Dixie bent down and patted me.

'Well, Izzie, we did well, we were the best we could be, well done. I don't think we'll have such a hair-raising flight next time!'

As I sat there with Dixie by my side, I recalled my life as a stray in Dublin and how I was selected to be trained as a Hearing Dog, before failing their two-star test. I didn't realise it at the time, but that door closing led to another, more exiting adventure as a space dog. I had achieved a lot, I thought. Moments like this are special. I wagged my tail happily.

'Treat?' I woofed hopefully.

Have you read the other books in the Izzie series?
Royalties are donated to Hearing Dogs for Deaf People.
Available from Amazon Books.

A Small Dog Story

Based on true events, enjoy the story of Izzie the dog, a little terrier, big in personality. Born in Dublin, lost as a puppy, find out how she survives as a stray with the help of friends she meets along the way, and from Benni the streetwise dog. Her adventures include life in Dublin, how she is chosen as a Hearing Dog and her travels to England for training. Humorous, hopeful and happy. Woof!

Izzie and the Martian Adventure

Izzie's 'pack' are astronauts, and she earns the chance to be a specialist space dog. At the Space Academy, she is faced with the mystery of the secret ion drive theft, but tough training and more assessments lie ahead. A tragic event leads to a journey to Mars with Dixie, her handler, where a bigger, more sinister mystery awaits. But are her skills up to the job? Can she help stop the criminal mastermind before it is too late? Does she really have a doggy spacesuit? And are there any squirrels in space?

Thanks

Thanks to my wife Sally, who supported me when writing this book. She is a natural editor and made many suggestions and gave me some great ideas. She also insisted I read the writing notes she had put together for her children at school.

Thanks to my daughter, Sarah, a primary school teacher, who drew Izzie in her spacesuit and carried out the final proofread.

The other sketches of Izzie were drawn by Grandma Shirley, who loved animals.

Lastly, thanks to those who bought Izzie's first two books and gave me positive feedback, which encouraged me on. At the time of writing, we have raised over £565 for Hearing Dogs for Deaf People, through the sale of Izzie's books.

Printed in Poland
by Amazon Fulfillment
Poland Sp. z o.o., Wrocław

65082517R00103